KT-176-278

3 8014 05118 2951

The Man from Cheyenne

The last man to wear a sheriff's badge had finally been driven out of Jackson Creek. Jake Pierce was aiming higher than the profits from his Silver Lode saloon and, backed by a group of vicious gunfighters, he was planning to take over the town.

So when Clay Harding rides from Cheyenne to bring back the rule of law he is sucked into a whirlpool of killing and the lure of gold. Knowing that he might never get back to Cheyenne he could console himself with one thought: with his faithful Colt in his hand he might just shoot his way out of trouble. . . .

By the same author

Lannigan's Star
Stage to Cheyenne
Shadow of the Gun
Wyoming Showdown
Storm over Wyoming
Trail to Fort Laramie
Bear Creek

The Man from Cheyenne

Jack Edwardes

A Black Horse Western

ROBERT HALE · LONDON

© Jack Edwardes 2012
First published in Great Britain 2012

ISBN 978-0-7090-9568-2

Robert Hale Limited
Clerkenwell House
Clerkenwell Green
London EC1R 0HT

www.halebooks.com

The right of Jack Edwardes to be identified as
author of this work has been asserted by him
in accordance with the Copyright, Designs and
Patents Act 1988

Typeset by
Derek Doyle & Associates, Shaw Heath
Printed and bound in Great Britain by
CPI Antony Rowe, Chippenham and Eastbourne

CHAPTER ONE

Clay Harding watched the dying embers of his morning fire. Its flames, sheltered by the cottonwoods around him, had kept him warm during the cold Wyoming night and heated the pan of beans he'd eaten for breakfast.

He looked across to the other side of the fire where his buckskin was nibbling at the bunch and buffalo grass. He'd bought the buckskin at a stagecoach station a few miles east of Cheyenne after his roan had broken a leg in a jackrabbit hole. The buckskin wasn't what he'd wanted but it was the only mount for sale and he'd buy another horse for the return journey to Cheyenne.

As if aware it was being studied, the buckskin raised its head and turned amber-coloured eyes in Harding's direction. Although it needed feeding up, the animal was a good horse, ideal for the Army. But it was too small for him. Harding grinned, suddenly remembering that day back East in '63 when he'd tried to join the cavalry. The recruiting sergeant, a Dutchman with fine moustaches had looked at him across the desk and shaken his head.

''No chance,' he'd said.

'I'm not after being an officer,' Harding remembered telling him.

The Dutchman had snorted. 'I'm sure you ain't. But just

how tall are you?'

'Six feet two.'

'Then, young feller, you wanna fight with the cavalry I'm gonna haveta saw six inches off you,' the Dutchman had said. 'No more than five eight for the cavalry.'

He'd walked out of the room feeling foolish and racking his brains for a notion of what to do next. His father had been furious after he'd written to say he was quitting college to go to the War. Only when he'd returned home after the Confederacy had surrendered, and he took off his blue uniform for what he thought was the last time did he discover that his father had followed every movement of the 132nd Pennsylvania Volunteers. A framed newspaper clipping hung in the parlour recording his brevet promotion to captain after the battle at South Mountain. His father was even more pleased when he learned his son was going back to law school. Harding's mouth twitched. He'd travelled a hard road since those days. He spoke aloud to the buckskin. 'I guess it was all for the best.'

That was the moment when he heard shouting and a woman's voice raised in anger and then again with a tinge of fear. Harding came off the ground like an uncoiled spring, throwing the dregs of his coffee over the smouldering embers. He stamped down hard to extinguish the fire, and six long strides took him to his mount. Moments later the buckskin was weaving its way through the trees, and as he reached the end of the stand, Harding was able to look down on the river.

In the middle of the shallow waters, at the point where he'd forded the river the evening before, a buggy, pulled by a single horse, appeared to be stuck firm. The driver, a fat man, his face red, was urging the animal on with his long whip. Alongside the driver sat a young woman wearing a fashionable green coat and a small hat over her auburn hair.

Despite the horse's efforts the buggy remained stuck, water lapping around the wheel axles. Harding guessed that the weight of the two people and the pile of boxes strapped to the rear of the buggy had sunk the wheels into the mud of the river-bed. He touched the sides of his buckskin, leaning back in the saddle as he rode down the slope, then reining in when he'd reached the river-bank and drawn level with the buggy.

'You folks need any help?' Harding called.

'I'm sure Mr Baskins can manage by himself,' the voice of the young woman, her head held high, was cold.

'Mighty friendly of you, sir!' cailed Baskins. 'We'll—'

He broke off, and the young woman gave a little scream as the buggy suddenly dropped several inches deeper into the water, tilting sideways and threatening to throw both driver and passenger into the river.

'What in tarnation happened there?' Baskins called, as both he and the young woman clutched at the side of the buggy.

'I guess you must be in some sort of mudhole,' Harding called. 'It's too late to use my buckskin; she's not strong enough. Best if you step out, Mr Baskins. I'll come in after you if you have any trouble getting to the bank.'

The young woman's voice went up an octave. 'Baskins! You are not to leave me here!'

Harding couldn't hide his grin. 'Then ma'am, are you gonna try it?'

'I am certainly not!'

Harding touched the buckskin's sides, urging the animal into the water to splash across the ten or fifteen yards until he could draw alongside the buggy. With the early sun behind him he could see the young woman more clearly as she turned to face him. She had green eyes. Irish stock, maybe, Harding thought.

7

'OK, ma'am, I want you to stand up.'

She looked at Baskins who nodded encouragement. Gripping the side of the buggy she rose slowly to her feet. Harding moved the buckskin a couple of feet closer to the buggy. He leaned sideways, his arm shooting out and around the waist of the young woman. Ignoring her protests, he flexed his arm muscles, tightened his grip, and with a sudden heave lifted her from the buggy on to the saddle in front of him. Their heads were only inches apart, and she strained away from him.

'How dare you! How dare you manhandle me!'

Harding ignored her, his mouth curving in a smile before he addressed the driver. 'You could try and get moving again. If needs be I'll come back for the boxes and that should fix things.'

The young woman struggled to sit upright, her hand grasping the horn of the buckskin's saddle. 'Mr Baskins! Don't just sit there and leave me with this ruffian!'

Before Baskins had a chance to reply, Harding turned the buckskin's head and headed for the bank. Maybe he shouldn't have been too surprised at the reaction of the young woman who was still struggling to put as much space as possible between them. After days on the trail, he needed a shave, a bath and a change of clothes. He probably didn't smell too good, unlike his unwilling passenger who gave off a scent of wild flowers.

'As soon as we're on the bank you're to put me down,' she said curtly.

'Sure, ma'am.'

The buckskin splashed out of the water, head bobbing, as it laboured up the muddy slope. Harding was tempted to offload the young woman into the mud as she'd ordered but decided against it. She almost certainly lived in Jackson Creek and maybe he'd have the chance to meet her again.

They reached the grass just as a triumphant shout from Baskins told them that the buggy had broken free.

Harding leaned back in the saddle, holding out his arm to enable the young woman to step down to the ground.

'Thank you,' she said shortly, not looking at him.

Harding put a finger to the brim of his Stetson. 'My pleasure, ma'am. I guess you'll be fine now with Mr Baskins.'

Without waiting for an answer he turned the buckskin's head and with a raised hand to acknowledge the shout of gratitude from Baskins he headed back to the trail.

The morning sun on his face made for easy riding and he reckoned that if he kept his mount at a steady trot, maybe resting after a couple of hours for ten minutes or so, he'd reach Jackson Creek by noon. The town would be quiet then, which would give him time to size up the place, and get the feeling of what he was going up against. He'd been warned in Cheyenne that he could be in for a rough ride, and any help he called for would be three or four days away. His mouth twitched. Hell, it wasn't the first time he'd played a poor hand and picked up the winnings. Not with a deck of cards though, he thought wryly.

'What the hell!'

His shout cut through the clear air. The crack of a long gun reached his ears as blood spurted from the side of the buckskin's head. Harding felt the horse going from beneath him. He kicked out of his stirrups rolling from the saddle, and slamming against the hard ground of the trail, jarring every bone in his body. His Colt dug painfully into his hip as he scrabbled across the ground using the carcass of the dead horse for protection against the chance of more shots from the hidden gunman.

His eyes swept the distant stand of trees for any sign of approaching men. Breathing deeply, he pulled his Winchester from its scabbard and fired off a couple of shots

9

in the direction of the cottonwoods over to his right. He didn't expect to hit anything aside from trees but it might give him a chance to reckon how many men he was up against if more shots were fired. Then he heard the distant beat of a single horse's hoofs fading into the distance.

He scrambled to his feet. Around the bend in the trail and heading towards him was the buggy carrying the passengers he'd helped at the river. He wouldn't have to walk, after all. He stood by the dead horse watching them approach. Baskins pulled back on the reins, bringing the buggy to a halt. He and the young woman stared down at the dead animal.

'What in tarnation happened here?' Baskins said.

Harding thought for a second. There was no point in showing his cards before he'd even reached Jackson.

'Horse broke his leg in a prairie-dog's hole. I had to shoot him.'

'Yeah, thought I heard a coupla shots. If Miss Dawson has no objections you're welcome to ride along with us.'

'You're welcome, Mr—?'

'Name's Harding, ma'am. I'm obliged to you.'

Baskins settled his whip. 'I'll give you a hand with your rig.' He stepped down and together he and Harding began to free the cinch, then both of them heaved at the saddle flap to free it from beneath the dead horse.

'Are you heading for Jackson, Mr Harding?' Baskins asked, a little out of breath from his efforts.

Harding paused, setting his saddle on top of the boxes at the rear of the buggy. 'That's right, Mr Baskins. I've work to do there.'

'I hope you're not working for that ruffian Jake Pierce,' the young woman snapped, turning around, her face taut.

Harding smiled grimly. 'No, ma'am. I'm the town's new sheriff.'

CHAPTER TWO

'I gotta say, Mr Harding, I'm mighty glad you're in town.'

Mayor Walter Bannon shook Harding's hand vigorously, as if pumping water. The black patches beneath his eyes showed sleepless nights, and Bannon's free hand trembled slightly.

'Take a seat.' Bannon waved a hand in the direction of a plain wooden chair as he moved to sit behind his desk. 'I run the hotel and the town from this office. Or mebbe I should say,' he added bitterly, 'I useta run this town.'

'What have you told the townsfolk?'

'We needed a sheriff, an' I rode to Cheyenne an' hired one. That's all, an' it ain't too far from the truth.'

'None of the townsfolk willing to stand?'

Bannon shook his head. 'I don't hold it against the men with families. Bein' sheriff the way we are now is a dangerous business. Coupla men without wives came forward afore winter. They ain't even in town no more. No-goods of Pierce ran 'em off.'

'Any deputies?'

Again Bannon shook his head. 'No. Seb Haines helps out around the jailhouse but he's got a peg leg and one eye missin'.'

'What's the pay for a deputy if I can find one?'

11

'Thirty a month. I'm told Cheyenne's payin' you.'

'Make it fifty for the deputy. He's gonna be puttin' his life on the line.'

Bannon hesitated for moment but then nodded. 'OK. Fifty.'

'So who looked after the town this last winter?'

Bannon looked out of the window for a couple of seconds before turning back to Harding. 'Nobody,' he said heavily. 'Only the weather saved us, or Jake Pierce woulda taken over Jackson an' brought in even more gunslingers, whores and gamblers.'

Harding got to his feet. 'Guess I'll find a good boarding house, and then take a look in the sheriff's office.'

'I can spare a room here, tho' there's a clapboard next to the sheriff's office that goes with the badge. Last feller wasn't that fancy but it'll clean up.'

'I'll take a look at it. First, I need the dry goods store.'

'Fifty yards past the livery. Left-hand side.' Bannon frowned. 'I see you ain't wearin' the badge yet.'

'I'll take a look around the town first.' Harding gave a grim smile. 'Folks'll know who I am soon enough.'

The watery afternoon sun was shedding its pale light on the town as Harding left the Bannon Hotel and crossed Main Street. Some of the men he passed on the boardwalks glanced at the Navy Colt on his hip, as if trying to guess his reason for coming to their town. Three men were lounging on high-backed chairs in front of the Silver Lode saloon and he was aware of their glares and the muttered words they exchanged as he walked past.

A couple of minutes later he reached the dry goods store, a large single-storey building built with timbers hewn from logs that suggested the store could have been built when Jackson was first settled. The scents of new silks and cottons reached Harding as he stepped through the open doorway.

The town, he realized, had been established long enough for a fair number of women to be living thereabouts.

Ahead of him, behind a long wooden counter, a youngster stood polishing a brass lamp. Beside him a lean board-hard man around fifty with curling moustaches was serving two women, their backs to the door. The storekeeper looked up from a bolt of cloth over the shoulders of the women.

'Be with you in a moment, sir.'

One of the women turned around slowly, and Harding casually glanced in her direction as he stepped further into the store. Then he stopped in his tracks as he recognized the young woman he'd rescued from the river. Her green eyes held Harding's gaze for a second before looking away. As the other woman, much older, turned to look Harding's way he raised his hand to remove his Stetson.

'Howdy, ladies.'

'My daughter tells me you were of great assistance to her this morning, Mr Harding.'

He realized then that the young woman must have spotted him entering Bannon's hotel to speak with the mayor. 'I just happened to be around, ma'am.'

'That's as maybe, but you gave aid when it was needed, and we both thank you.' She placed a hand on her daughter's arm. 'Come along, my dear. This gentleman has business with Mr Fielding.' With a nod in Harding's direction, she swept out of the store, her daughter a pace behind. The young woman's smile was friendlier than he'd expected. Harding was left with his hand half raised.

'I guess you're the feller from Cheyenne,' the storekeeper said. 'The mayor's been talkin' about you. Don't see no badge.'

'Tomorrow, Mr Fielding. I'm just looking around for a while.'

13

Fielding glanced at Harding's Navy Colt. 'Hope to heck you know how to use that. You're gonna need it, I guess.'

'I try not to use it, Mr Fielding.' Harding smiled. 'The two ladies who were here. You know them well? She's a mighty fine lookin' woman.'

'Mrs Henrietta Dawson sure is.' Fielding chuckled at Harding's expression. 'But I guess you're talkin' about her daughter, Miss Amy. They're fine folks an' they're a coupla brave ladies, keep goin' without a man.'

'How d'you mean?'

'Old John Dawson made a heap of money when he sold the bank and retired. But he lost three sons in the War an' he was never the same. Then two years back the cholera took him off. Word has it the Dawson money ain't so plentiful nowadays. Folks say that Henrietta Dawson's trips to Cheyenne are to sell her jewellery. Then a coupla weeks back an English feller who was payin' to stay at the Dawsons' place got his head broken on a rock when he was thrown from his horse. Some folks said it musta been Jake Pierce's work but that don't make much sense.'

'Seems everyone's talking of Pierce.'

Fielding shrugged. 'He's said to be runnin' for mayor next year. I'll own he's a neat lookin' feller. Fancy clothes, handmade boots, diamond ring on his pinkie. Them big cigars he's allus smokin'.' Fielding spat noisily into a spittoon. 'He's a ruthless sonovabitch, an' handy with a gun. He's gonna ruin this town with his gamblers an' whores. But plenty of folks are willin' to stand back while he's makin' 'em money.'

'Not everyone, Mr Fielding!'

Harding turned quickly. Amy Dawson stood framed in the doorway, the sunlight creating a reddish glow around her head. She stepped into the store.

'Jake Pierce is only one man, Mr Fielding,' she said. 'A

14

better man will surely bring him down.'

She picked up a small box from a table. 'Mother forgot her cottons,' she said. She turned to look directly at Harding, her eyes sparkling, although whether with anger or friendliness, Harding wasn't sure.

'Gentlemen,' she said, with a slight inclination of her head. Then with a flurry of her skirts she was gone, leaving the two men staring after her.

Fielding broke the silence. 'Jackson Creek sure needs more like her.'

'The town looks good to me.'

'Yeah, like a shiny red apple,' Fielding said. 'All ready for pluckin'. An' Pierce is soon gonna be reachin'.' The store-keeper shook his head as if to rid himself of troubled thoughts. 'Anyways, Mr Harding, what can I sell you? You wanna order anythin' special I got a wagon comin' in next week from the railroad down south.'

'I just need a coupla shirts.'

'Somethin' fancy for the shindig tonight?'

'First I've heard of it.'

'Down at the Old Barn, back of the livery. Whole town'll be there. You might wanna wear the badge.'

Harding nodded. 'Good thinkin', Mr Fielding.'

Fielding pointed across the store to a pile of boxes. 'Plenty o' shirts over there.'

Harding was paying for a couple of work shirts and one with fancy trimming he planned to wear that evening when behind him came a shout of excitement and a beanpole of a man wearing bib coveralls came dashing into the store.

'Better close your doors, Ben! There's gonna be another gunfight! Charlie Wilson's comin' down Main Street an' he's madder than a badger in a pig wallow!'

Harding dropped the shirts on to the counter, saying, 'I'll pick those up later.' Without waiting for an answer he turned on his heel and strode out of the store on to the boardwalk to take a long look at the grim-faced young man striding down the centre of Main Street.

Harding stepped down to the hardpack. For fifty yards in either direction he and Wilson were the only two in Main Street. The townsfolk must have guessed what could happen and had scattered to the boardwalks. Harding's stare never left the approaching Wilson. From both sides of the street came the sound of men ordering their women and children to keep out of sight. When Wilson was ten yards away Harding held up his hand.

'Hold it there, Mr Wilson. I reckon we need to talk.'

Wilson's mouth was set in a grim line. 'I don't know you, mister, but you'd be wise to get out of my way.'

'Tomorrow you'll see me wearing the sheriff's badge. That's if you're still alive. What you aimin' to do?'

'What the hell's it got to do with you?'

Harding shrugged. 'Nothin', I reckon. But I ain't of a mind to see a man killed on this fine spring day.'

'That sidewinder Pierce put his hands on my little sister. I'm gonna kill him for doin' that.'

'I hear Pierce is handy with a gun.'

Wilson spat in the dust. 'An' he's gonna find out I'm faster.'

Harding looked thoughtful. 'Is that right? How about showin' me?'

Wilson pulled his lips back on to his teeth. 'I ain't drawing on no lawman even if you ain't wearing no badge.'

'Hell! I ain't asking you to shoot me! I just wanna see how fast you are.'

Wilson didn't hesitate. His hand flashed to the butt of his sidearm. His Savage revolver was inches out of its holster when he froze, staring down the barrel of Harding's Navy Colt aimed directly between his eyes. From the boardwalk

16

came an excited chatter of voices.

'Did you jest see that!'

Harding paused for a moment before lowering his arm and reholstering his Colt. 'You ain't bad,' he said. 'Mebbe you ain't as fast as you think you are.'

He looked over to his right. 'The Chinaman's open. What say I buy you a coffee?'

Wilson slowly slid his sidearm back in its holster, his face red. 'You joshin' me?' he snapped.

Harding shook his head. 'No, I ain't, Mr Wilson. I just wanna know more about what happened to your sister.'

Wilson hesitated for a moment. Then he nodded. 'OK, but I don't have a cent for coffee.'

'I said it's on me. C'mon, or folks'll be wonderin' what we're about.'

Harding turned on his heel, and headed for the board-walk, Wilson stepping out to keep up with him.

'OK, folks. Fun's all over. Me and Mr Wilson are gonna get coffee.'

The townsfolk backed away, the chatter of their voices loud in the still air of the afternoon.

'Who the heck is he?' A grey-haired old-timer asked loudly.

Harding pushed open the door of the Chinaman's place, and a few moments later the two men were sitting at a table. In front of them were steaming mugs of strong black coffee.

'OK, let's hear what you haveta say,' Harding said.

Wilson chewed at his lip for a moment, appearing to gather his thoughts.

'Our gran'pappy was sick this winter. He was real bad. Doc Radman had to send to Cheyenne for medicines an' stuff. The sawbone's a good man but he don't work for nothin'. We needed fifty dollars we hadn't got. Pierce got to know how we were fixed. Afore I could stop her, Lucy, my

17

sister, had borrowed the money from Pierce. He's got her workin' in the Lode afore she pays it back.'

'You mean as a calico queen?'

Wilson reacted as if stung. 'No, sir! She wouldn't do that. He had her sewing things an' stuff. Then he got her skivvying in the back room. That's where he put his dirty hands on her. If Pierce's wife hadn't walked in on 'em—' His voice trailed away and he turned away from Harding.

'So what's your part in all this? Why don't you work off the debt?'

'Cos nobody'll give me work. I'm flat busted.' Wilson's mouth twisted. 'You'll hear soon enough. My mother was a whore an' my father the town drunk. Decent folks think I'm like 'em, but I ain't.'

'Jackson's not the only town in the Territory.'

Wilson shook his head. 'Gran'pappy's too old to move now. An' Lucy an' me owe him too much to leave him. Him an' gran'ma looked after us when I was still in britches and stockin's, an' Lucy in a diaper.'

Harding took a sip of his coffee, studying Wilson over the rim of his mug.

'Can you read and write?'

Wilson bridled at the question. 'Sure I can! Gran'pappy taught Lucy an' me real well.'

'You gotta horse?'

Wilson shrugged. 'She ain't much use. Too old for anythin', but I got a good rig on her.'

Harding reached for the inside pocket of his leather vest and pulled out several bills. He pushed them across the table. 'OK, go on up to the livery stable an' get yourself a good mount. Get rid o' that Savage, and get yourself a Colt. Then go home. Be at the sheriff's office an hour after sunup.'

Wilson's face showed his confusion. 'You're givin' me

money, an' tomorrow you're gonna put me in jail?'

'I'm gonna make you my deputy. You let me down, you can forget Pierce; I'll be the one chasin' you.'

'Jumpin' rattlesnakes!' Wilson's face beamed with pleasure. Then his smile was wiped in an instant. 'But I still gotta see about Lucy.'

'Leave her to me. No sense in gettin' yourself shot up afore you've even been sworn in. I'll see Pierce.' Harding drained the last of his coffee, and stood up looking down on Wilson. 'I'm taking a chance on you. Remember what I said about letting me down.'

The Silver Lode was one of the dozen two-storey buildings in the town and bigger within than Harding had expected. The bar ran several yards along the wall to his left, finishing in a curve before two doors alongside each other set in the stucco wall. In front of the bar, stretching across the width of the room, tables and chairs were scattered by four long tables covered in green baize.

At the far end of the room was a small stage where, Harding guessed, musicians would play when the crowd was in. To the right of the stage beyond another door, a curved set of stairs led up to the rooms where the calico queens would carry on their business. Somewhere up there, he assumed, were private rooms for Pierce.

At this time of day the place was almost deserted. A single figure, sipping his beer, stood at the end of the bar opposite the barkeeper, a Mexican, by his features. Four men were at a table, one of them stylishly dressed in a black coat with fancy trimmings on the lapels. Pierce maybe? Behind him sat a woman, her attention on the cards. The four men looked Harding's way as he approached the bar but then concentrated on the cards in their hands.

The Mexican moved along the bar towards him. 'What is

your pleasure, *señor?*'

'I'll take a beer.'

'That'll be two bits, *señor.*'

'Put that on the house, Ramón.'

A woman spoke behind Harding. He turned to see the woman he'd noticed behind the card-player. She was maybe in her late thirties. A blue skirt fell to the top of her shoes. Above the skirt her shoulders were covered with a blue shirt, its sleeves buttoned at her wrists. No calico queen, Harding decided, but certainly no lady, her assured expression showing she was comfortable with being in the saloon.

'You sure have changed,' she said. 'Last time I saw you, Mr Harding, you were in a city suit and a derby hat.'

How did this woman know his name? 'I don't think—'

'Don't you remember me? I ain't likely to forget ten years back you saved me from swingin' at the end of a rope in a Pennsylvania prison.'

'Beth Maynard! My God! You were my first case!'

'An' you were all I could afford!'

Harding smiled. She was right. His fees were low when he was first starting out. 'How come you're out West?'

'I've been here a while. I'm Mrs Jake Pierce now. All signed and legal.'

Did he detect a shadow in her eyes as she said that? Maybe his imagination was working overtime. After all, it was a long time since he'd last seen her.

'So what brings you to Jackson Creek, Mr Harding?'

'I'm takin' over as sheriff,' he said, and ignored her startled look. 'Right now I need to see Lucy Wilson.'

'She's in the back room. First door at the end of the bar. Shall I—?'

'No need. I can find her myself.'

He didn't wait for her reply, but turned on his heel and headed along the bar, aware that behind him Beth Pierce's shoes were sounding on the wooden floor as she headed rapidly back to the card players.

He pushed open the door at the end of the bar and stepped into a windowless room. Steam rose from pans of hot water standing around on the stone floor. At the centre of the room a young woman dressed in a dirty grey smock was bent over a large metal bowl scrubbing at a greasy pan. She didn't look up as he stepped forward, her long blonde hair shielding her expression.

'Lucy Wilson?' Harding said quietly.

The girl looked up and Harding realized she was aged no more than fifteen or sixteen. Despite her face being ashen with fatigue he could see that she was a pretty girl, with even features, a well-shaped nose, and blue eyes.

'Your brother sent me. I'm takin' you out of this place.'

She managed a sad smile. 'When did Charlie ever have thirty dollars?'

'Don't you worry about that. Charlie's lookin' out for you. He wants you back with your gran'pappy. You ready to go?'

'Mister, I don't know you but if Charlie sent you with thirty dollars that's fine by me.' She threw the dirty cloth into the pan, and dried her hands on a rag. 'I was scared that Charlie would do somethin' stupid.'

'OK, you stay behind me an' we'll see Pierce.'

Her head jerked up. 'I ain't gonna see that pig Pierce.'

'OK, you don't haveta. Leave that to me.'

He turned on his heel and went back into the saloon, Lucy trailing behind him. As they walked the length of the bar Harding was conscious of the four men putting down their cards and staring across at them. He reached the end of the bar and turned to the girl.

'You stand here, Lucy. I'll settle this with Pierce.'

'I don't know what the hell you think you're doin', Harding,' called the man wearing the fancy black jacket.

21

'But I'm damned sure that gal ain't goin' nowhere.'

Harding was silent until he reached the table. The four men looked up at him, with half-smiles which didn't reach their eyes.

'Lookit here, boss. Sheriff come for his pay-off. Ain't been in town ten minutes.'

The dark-complexioned man to Pierce's right sniggered at his own joke, looking around the table for approval.

Harding looked at him. 'I hear you talkin' agin about bribing a lawman an' you'll be breakin' rocks down in Cheyenne,' he said evenly.

'Why you—!'

Pierce's hand shot out to prevent the chair being kicked back. 'Take it easy, Frenchie. The man's only doin' his job.' He looked up at Harding. 'But that don't mean you can bust in here and start orderin' my people around.' He took the cigar from the tray in front of him and pointed it across the saloon. 'An' that includes little Lucy.'

'She's workin' here cos she owes you money.'

'That's right, Mr Harding. An' she'll stay here until I see all of my fifty dollars. She still owes me thirty.'

Harding reached into his vest pocket, and took out a sheaf of bills. He leaned forward between two of the men and tossed the money on to the table. 'Thirty dollars,' he said. 'She's walkin' out with me now.'

'An' if I say I made a mistake an' meant to say thirty-five?'

'I'd say you were a four-flusher, an' I'll take her out for nothin'.'

Harding's left hand shot out between the two men and scooped up the money. Pierce wasn't quick enough a second time to stop the dark-complexioned Frenchie from kicking back his chair and dropping his hand to the butt of his gun.

'You wanna die over thirty dollars?' barked Harding at him. 'You draw that sidearm an' I'll kill you.' He stared hard

22

at the no-good. Nobody around the table moved an inch. Slowly, Frenchie took his hand from his sidearm and sat down, his face burning with pent-up rage.

'You play a hard game, Mr Harding,' Pierce said. 'Jest make sure it don't come back to bite you.'

'I've been playin' a hard game fer a long time, Mr Pierce. I watch out fer snakebites. I'm tellin' you all now. The next man who puts a hand on a woman without her say-so will be pickin' hemp in Cheyenne Prison.' Harding looked around the table. 'I came in here peaceful, an' I'm aimin' to leave that way. Take the thirty dollars, let the girl go, an' know that from noon today Jackson's a law-abidin' town agin.'

He threw the bills back on to the table, nodded at Beth Pierce and put a finger to the brim of his hat. 'Good to see you again, Mrs Pierce.' He took another look around, and satisfied, turned his back on the table.

'Let's get you outa here, Lucy,' he called.

CHAPTER THREE

'We're gonna walk across to the clapboard next to the sheriff's office,' Harding said as he pushed through the batwing doors of the saloon and stepped out on to the boardwalk.

'I ain't goin' anywhere with you,' Lucy said defiantly. 'I don't know you, and I want to see Charlie. Them thirty dollars don't mean you've bought me like some calico queen in the Lode. Anyways, that clapboard belongs to the sheriff when we have one.'

Harding grinned; Lucy sure had spirit. 'Relax, Lucy. I am the sheriff.'

'Where's your badge? I don't see no badge.'

Harding breathed in deeply. Maybe he should have nailed the badge to his forehead. He reached into his vest pocket. 'Here, you believe me now?'

'Oh my! I thought you was—' Her voice trailed away for a moment. 'Well, you know, comin' into the Lode an' flashin' that money. I don't believe Charlie gave it you at all.'

'You're right, Lucy. A very important man down in Cheyenne gave it to me.'

Ignoring her puzzled expression he led the way down the steps and together they crossed Main Street and walked the fifty yards to the sheriff's office and the little clapboard house alongside it.

'Why you takin' me here?' Lucy said, a suspicious tone remaining in her voice.

'Can you keep a good house?'

For the first time since Harding had seen her, Lucy gave a wide smile.

'Gran'pappy says I keep the best house in the county, an' he knows from when he worked for a real English gentleman.'

'OK, so let's take a look.'

He opened the door of the clapboard, and the smell hit both of them as strong as a prairie wind. The gagging stink of rotting food, the aroma of cheap whiskey mixed with the scent of strong tobacco and human sweat caused them both to screw up their faces in disgust.

'If you're gonna live here there's a lotta work to do,' Lucy said.

'So how would you like to look after this house? I could pay you, say, twenty dollars a month.'

Lucy began to smile broadly but then looked up at him from beneath a suspicious frown. 'That's a lotta money. There ain't anything more to it than that? Keepin' house, I mean.'

Harding grimaced, his patience strained. 'Yes, there darned well is! Afore you start here you go home an' get a good bath. Cut that mop of hair, and wash that smock you're wearin'.' He pulled out a handful of coins from his pants pocket. 'You go and see Mr Fielding an' buy yourself a coupla work-dresses, an' somethin' you can wear to church on Sunday.'

He thrust the coins into her hand, and waved her away. 'Be here an hour after sunup an' don't be late,' he called out as she tripped down the short path.

As she reached the small gate she turned to look back at

him. 'I don't go to church, Sheriff Harding, but I'll wear it tonight and have all the boys wanting to dance with me.'

Harding couldn't hide his grin. 'You're an impudent brat. Then don't get too tired. I want to see this place as bright as a new pin tomorrow.'

Several hours later Harding had picked up his shirts from Fielding, paid a visit to the bathhouse, shaved, and arranged for the jacket and pants he was carrying in his saddle-bag to be sponged and pressed by the one of the maids at Bannon's where he'd arranged a room for a couple of nights.

Now, while late afternoon settled on the town he made his way to the Old Barn. As he walked along the boardwalk, several of the townsfolk greeted him warmly as if pleased to see someone at last wearing the sheriff's star. Others eyed him suspiciously, as if a stranger from Cheyenne, sheriff or not, could only mean that he was in the pay of Jake Pierce.

He followed a group of young men who, by the noise they were making, were keen on having a good time, and maybe planning to sneak a couple of glasses of strong punch if their seniors weren't watching too closely. He stepped into the barn, which had been dressed up like it was the Fourth of July, the walls of the barn fixed with candle-holders throwing a soft yellow light on to the large number of townsfolk already in attendance.

'Howdy, Sheriff Harding. Welcome to Jackson Creek.'

The speaker was tall, red-faced and sported mutton-chop whiskers. His checked coat covered a white silk shirt over a dark blue vest. Around his neck was a large bow tie, which flopped on to his shirt front. He thrust out a hand.

'Hector Housman,' he introduced himself. 'I run the town's newspaper, the *Clarion*. I'll be running a piece on you, this week, Mr Harding.'

'Don't write too much of the truth, Mr Housman.'

Housman threw back his head and laughed. 'You folks from Cheyenne are mighty smart. How long since you left there?'

'Coupla weeks.'

'Tell me. Did you see any of Lotta Crabtree, "The Nation's Darling"? Folks reckon she has the crowds cheering.'

'I saw her show three times, an' then met her later.'

For a moment Harding thought Housman was about to manhandle him, such was his reaction. 'Did you indeed, Mr Harding? Then you must give me your views on the beautiful Lotta. I'd ask Miss Dawson but mebbe Lotta Crabtree ain't right for a lady. I can promise you a full column. Just the impression you'll wish to make now you're in town.'

'I'll do that, Mr Housman,' he looked around. 'I'm hopin' to speak with Miss Dawson.'

'Be warned! She has this notion about the Englishman, Robert Dale. But I'm sure she'd wish to thank you for your kindness at the river.'

'Seems word gets 'round fast in Jackson, Mr Housman.'

Harding made his escape, returning greetings from several of the townsmen as he made his way along the length of the barn. Finally, he arrived within speaking distance of Amy Dawson, who sat with her mother and an older man.

'Good evening, ladies, and you, sir,' he said, inclining his head in the man's direction.

'Good evening, Sheriff,' Mrs Dawson said. 'You haven't yet met Mr Reece who runs the town's bank.'

Reece stood up and shook Harding's hand. 'You'll need to be strong, Mr Harding.' He nodded in the direction of the opposite side of the barn. At a large table, half a dozen men surrounded Jake Pierce and his wife. 'But you'll know all about that, I guess.' He looked down at the older woman. 'Henrietta, may I offer you some of the delicious fruit punch?'

27

'You may, indeed, George.'

Mrs Dawson stood up and with a tilt of her head in Harding's direction took the proffered arm of the banker, leaving Amy Dawson alone with Harding.

'I hope you're fully rested from your travels, Miss Dawson.'

'Mr Harding, I think I'll scream if anyone asks me that question again.' She smiled, taking the sting from her words. 'I've been in Boston for the winter and I was not aware until then how stuffy we can sometimes be in the West.' She indicated the chair alongside her. 'Do sit down, and we'll scandalize the good ladies of the town.'

Harding grinned, and did as he was bid.

'Mr Housman tells me you write for the *Clarion?*'

'Notes on the history of the Territory, Mr Harding. Some in the town say they enjoy reading them.' But then he was surprised to see Amy Dawson's expression become serious. 'Mr Harding, there's something I must ask you.'

'Fire away, Miss Dawson.'

'Two weeks ago Mr Robert Dale, our house guest, was killed. It was said that his horse had trod into a prairie-dog's hole and thrown him. His lifeless body was found near the homesteads close to the river.'

Harding nodded. 'I've already heard about that.'

'Robert Dale was a small man but he was a fine horseman. He'd hunted the fox in England since he was twelve years old. Even the cowboys at the Green Valley ranch admired his riding.'

'Accidents happen to the best riders, Miss Dawson.'

'This was no accident, Mr Harding. I'm convinced of it. I think Mr Dale was murdered.'

Harding looked at her, recognizing in the set of her mouth that she was determined to make her suspicions plain to him. But that didn't make them well founded, he decided.

'I'm told he still had his timepiece and there was money in his pocket. Why would anyone wish to kill him?'

Amy Dawson hesitated. 'I don't know the answer to that.'

Harding shook his head. 'A man doesn't get killed for no reason, Miss Dawson.'

'For pity's sake, Mr Harding! That brute Jake Pierce must have had reason. Pierce is behind everything that's evil in this town.'

'Was Mr Dale planning on doing business here?'

'Not at all. He was a studious man. He was searching for certain rocks, trying to discover specimens that would make his name famous when he returned to England.'

'He was a miner?'

'No, no, he said there were important signs of animals and fish from long ago. He carried a book written by Mr Darwin, an Englishman. Mr Dale used to spend most days riding out to the homesteads. Then in the evenings he'd spend his time writing up his journal.'

'Miss Dawson, I'd been warned about Pierce before I left Cheyenne. He's a no-good but that doesn't make him a fool. Men like Pierce kill only for gain, and there's nothing to gain from the death of a man of books like your Mr Dale.' Harding stood up. 'I can't help, but it's been a pleasure sitting here with you.'

He gave a brief bow, ignoring the tightening of Amy Dawson's mouth, and moved away. One of the townsmen, who must have been waiting his chance, moved swiftly past him, and from the corner of his eye Harding saw the young man bow and heard him expressing the hope that Miss Dawson was fully rested from her travels.

After spending a few minutes with Mayor Bannon and thanking him for the free board and lodging Harding decided that it was time to leave. A stay of twenty minutes at an occasion like this was enough for him. Most of the townsfolk had seen him wearing the sheriff's badge, and that was good enough for an evening's work.

He caught a glimpse of Lucy surrounded by the young men who'd been ahead of him when he arrived. Fielding had obviously found for her the right sort of dress, and she must have slept since leaving the saloon. Her face was lit with a lovely smile as she first looked at one young man and then another. Harding looked around for Lucy's brother but Charlie Wilson wasn't in the barn. Maybe he was getting a good night's sleep.

'I see you've made the acquaintance of the town's belle,' a voice came from behind him. Harding turned to see Jake Pierce a few feet away. The cut of his stylish blue coat showed that it hadn't come from Jackson, not even from Cheyenne, but maybe from back East.

'It was my pleasure,' said Harding evenly.

'She tell you how I killed her English friend?'

'She spoke of it,' Harding admitted.

'Did you believe her?'

'I told her I couldn't help.'

'Good. Why would I want to kill a man who looked for old rocks?'

'That's what I told her. I explained that men like you only kill for money. Not for honour, not for courage, just for money.'

Pierce's face stiffened. 'Sheriff, you have a way of puttin' a notion that could anger a man.'

'So I've been told. Goodnight, Mr Pierce.'

Harding turned on his heel and headed for the door. Outside, the spring air felt crisp after the heat inside the barn. It had been pleasing to speak with Amy Dawson even if he'd been unable to help her.

His encounter with Jake Pierce had been interesting. He'd gained the impression that Pierce was anxious to show he had nothing to do with Dale's death. Why should he be so concerned? It was tempting to think that his own arrival as sheriff had made Pierce uneasy. It wasn't all that long ago when a sheriff in Wyoming Territory would hang a man merely on suspicion that he'd committed murder.

But those days were past and Harding dismissed the notion. Pierce must know that even if Harding brought him down, he'd face a judge. The enforcement of law in the Territory had come a long way since the War, but there was no question that Pierce had influence in Cheyenne. Somebody there had tipped him off that folks in Cheyenne were becoming uneasy about events in Jackson Creek. Otherwise, how would he have known when he, Harding, was arriving in Jackson, and attempt to kill him before he even reached the town?

He knew he'd have to give more thought—

His head exploded with a streak of light. The blow sent him to his knees, his hands instinctively thrusting forward to avoid hitting the hardpack with his face. Rough hands grabbed each wrist, pulling at his arms, and he went down, tasting dirt. A hoarse voice sounded close to his ear.

'You're gettin' this one warning, Harding. Get outa town or you're gonna die in Jackson.'

He let out a muffled grunt as one of his assailants – there were four of them, Harding guessed – kicked hard into his chest, and Harding felt one of his ribs creak. Then he was released, and he heard their running feet as the men made their getaway.

Instinctively he reached for his Colt, only to realize his sidearm was in its belt on the dresser of the hotel. 'Don't expect to carry my Colt for a town party,' he muttered. He pushed himself on to his knees, a wave of nausea sweeping over him.

His chest and his head throbbed with pain but when his

fingers gently probed the side of his head they remained dry. He'd suffered a scalp wound once and it had bled like hell, so he guessed that his Stetson had saved him from a greater injury. His chest, where the no-good had booted him was more worrying. His fingers pressed hard against his ribs. Luckily, he could feel no movement, although by the morning he guessed that his upper body was going to be as blue as the summer sky over the Rocky Mountains.

Slowly, he got to his feet. He had maybe a couple of hundred yards to the hotel, and a short climb up the stairs to his room, his bed, and the end of his first day in Jackson Creek. When he'd told them in Cheyenne he was thinking of asking to go back East he hadn't even convinced himself. Now he was sure. But before he left Jackson Creek he'd clear Pierce and his no-goods from the town.

CHAPTER FOUR

The sun had been up for almost an hour when the board-walk door to the sheriff's door was opened. Charlie Wilson looked startled at the sight of Harding bent over his desk writing in his journal.

'I ain't late, Sheriff. I took real care to be here on time.'

Harding looked up from his journal. 'No, Charlie, you're not late. Lucy beat you to the mark, though. Caught me scraping off my beard.'

Charlie's expression showed relief. He pushed open the door behind him a little wider, and stood back. Harding half-rose from his chair, staring in the direction of the door.

'What the hell you got there, Charlie?'

'A dog,' Charlie said, appearing to be taken aback by Harding's reaction.

'I can see it's a dog! What the heck you been feedin' him?'

Charlie grinned. 'He is big, ain't he? Boss of the Green Valley owes gran'pappy a favour, an' he sends down meat. Bruno's an English bloodhound. Gran'pappy useta breed them when he worked for the Englishman, Moreton Frewen, over at Powder River.'

'I'm mighty pleased for your gran'pappy, Charlie, an' I'm sure Bruno is a fine animal. But what's he doin' here?'

'I reckon he'll be useful. Police agents in Europe use 'em to track the no-goods they got over there.'

Harding breathed in deeply. The Wilsons seemed to have their own share of crazy ideas. 'You ain't likely to be trackin' any no-goods, Charlie. Drunk cowboys on a Saturday night don't need much lookin' fer.' He picked up a sheet of paper from his desk. 'Anyways, first job for you. Mayor Bannon's made a list of those who haven't paid taxes to the town this winter. You go see 'em an' tell 'em to pay up.'

Charlie's face registered disappointment. 'Is that all I gotta do?'

'I ain't followin' you.'

'I thought we'd be doin' somethin' about Pierce an' his no-goods.'

'You mean like chargin' into the Lode and shootin' like you was aimin' to do the other day?'

Charlie looked sheepish. 'Yeah, somethin' like that.'

'We ain't livin' in a Ned Buntline story, Charlie. We're here as lawmen an' until we got enough for a judge to visit Jackson we make sure we enforce the law of the Territory in the right way.'

'Yeah, OK.' Charlie bit the corner of his mouth. 'Fergit my foolish talk, Mr Harding.' He appeared to remember something. 'I guess then you're gonna be seein' Josh Wake if he's able to talk.'

Harding frowned. 'Nobody's said anythin' about a Josh Wake.'

'He's one of the town's lawyers. He's a good man, not like that sleazy Miller who does Pierce's work. Some no-good attacked Mr Wake coupla weeks back. He's been with Doc Radman ever since. Word has it he's not gonna make it.'

'First day, an' you're doin' well, Charlie,' Harding said, to the obvious pleasure of the deputy. 'Anyways, I need to have a word with Radman.' He held up the mayor's list. 'You all ready to start?'

'Sure am.' Charlie crossed the office and picked up the sheet of paper listing the non-payers of the town tax. He frowned as he looked down at the names on the list.

'Some of these are gonna be real ornery.'

'Tell 'em if they don't pay, Bruno'll eat 'em for supper.'

'OK, Sheriff, you can put your undershirt back on. You're darned lucky from what you've told me,' Doctor Radman said, washing his hands in a tin bowl of steaming water. 'You've got enough muscle about you to save your ribs. I could put one of my potions on the bruises an' charge you a coupla dollars but I reckon you're too smart for that. They'll fade away with time.'

'An' the knock on the head?'

Radman shook his head. 'Whoever the no-goods were they didn't mean to kill you. I guess you got a warning of some sort.'

Harding pulled on his shirt and his leather vest. 'Reckon you're on the mark, Doc,' he said. 'Thanks for takin' a look at me. How much do I owe you?'

'Have this on me. I've a notion that I'm gonna be makin' money with you in town.'

Harding smiled grimly. 'I'm obliged to you, and mebbe you're right. You gonna let me see Mr Wake?'

'If you promise to take it real gentle. Josh's in a bad way. But if you talkin' with him helps catch the no-goods who attacked him, it's worth a try.' Radman gestured in the direction of a door to the side. 'Follow me in.'

Radman moved to the door, Harding close behind, and the two men stepped into the sickroom. Against a wall, a single bunk held a man lying on his back, grey-white linen swathed around his head. His eyes were closed, his hands on the rough blanket were tightly clenched, and his breathing was unsteady.

'Josh,' Radman said softly, 'the new sheriff wants to have a word.' He nodded to Harding, who moved to stand alongside the injured lawyer.

'The name's Harding, Mr Wake. I'm gonna do my best to put the no-goods who attacked you in jail. You any idea who they were?' Harding asked gently.

Wake opened his eyes, his lips moving, but no words reached Harding's ears. He bent over to put his head closer to the lawyer's. 'Mr Wake, I need to know who attacked you,' he said, louder than before. He shifted to put his ear close to Wake's mouth.

'He was after the gold,' the lawyer managed to say. His eyes closed as if Wake had exhausted his energies with those few words.

Harding felt the doctor's hand on his shoulder. 'That's all, Mr Harding.'

'Did you hear what he said?'

Radman shook his head. 'Tell me outside. Let him sleep now.'

The two men left the room, the doctor closing the door to the sickroom behind them. 'Did he tell you who attacked him?'

Harding shook his head. 'No, Doc. Mr Wake said, an' I'm usin' his words now, "He was after the gold." '

Radman frowned. 'A head wound. A man can say anythin'. There's no gold around these parts. The Fremont expedition found coal thirty years ago but nothing came of it. You ride out to the homesteads an' you'll see the abandoned tunnels.'

'Could Mr Wake have gold stashed away in his home?'

'Josh dreamed of havin' a fancy office down in Cheyenne but he could never raise enough cash.' Radman shook his head. 'Josh doesn't have gold.'

'I guess you're right about the head wound. Anyways, Doc, I'm mighty grateful for your help.'

'You watch your back, Sheriff. There's a lot of good folk here but there's a lot of the other ones around Jackson.'

Heading back to his office Harding decided to stop off at the office of the *Clarion*. He guessed that Housman would give him no peace until he described his meeting with Lotta Crabtree. He hitched his horse at the rail outside the newspaper's office and pushed open the door marked with the paper's title.

Housman was standing by a large printing machine talking with a small elderly man wearing pince-nez who seemed intent on expressing to Housman his strong views on what was on the sheet of paper he was waving around in the air. Housman turned around as Harding paused at the doorway.

'Come through, Sheriff! I've been telling William here about your meeting with the beautiful protege of Lola Montez. William thinks it should make a full page.' His mouth twisted. 'A shame we couldn't show a real picture of La Belle Lotta. Mebbe one day. They're doing wonderful things back East.'

Housman pushed open the low wooden gate separating the printing area from a space occupied by a desk and a couple of chairs. With a sweep of his hand he indicated that Harding should take a seat. Housman picked up a pad of yellow paper and a pen from the inkwell on his desk. Behind him, William took off his ink-stained apron and leaned intently on the wooden gate, apparently anxious to hear every word.

'OK, you ready, Mr Housman?'

'At your service, Mr Harding.'

For the next hour Harding described his meeting with the toast of Cheyenne and, prompted by Housman, recalled his sitting alone for several minutes with this famous young woman who had swept across America like a shooting star. Finally, when Harding had run out of words and could think only of a glass of cold beer, Housman put down his pen.

'Splendid, Mr Harding. The paper will be sought after by every citizen of Jackson. I'm most grateful to you for grantin' me this favour.'

'Then maybe you can do one in return.'

'Anything, Sheriff. Just name it.'

'Would you look back in your files and check if there's any reference to gold?'

'I'll do that. The schoolmarm is always ready to earn a coupla dollars.' Housman's bushy eyebrows knitted together. 'But there's no gold in these parts, Mr Harding. There's coal out by the homesteads but there's no gold. But you've been mighty generous with your time, and I'll see the schoolmarm and put her to work once we've finished here.'

Harding took his leave, and moved along Main Street to the livery. The ex-cavalry trooper who owned the livery, Matt Parkes, had sold him a strong roan, and he'd decided to leave his new mount at the livery for the few months he planned to stay in Jackson. He asked Parkes to look after his rig, and then headed along the boardwalk in the direction of his office.

He was ten yards from the entrance of Bannon's when he spotted her. Amy Dawson was wearing a dark green jacket and a skirt of the same colour that brushed her shined button-shoes. Pinned atop her auburn hair was a small green hat with a tiny red feather. If Fielding at the store had been right about the Dawson women being short of funds, Amy Dawson was sure putting on a show. Harding stepped out, keen that she should see him before entering the hotel.

'Good morning, Miss Dawson. A fine morning.' His hand tugged briefly at the rim of his Stetson.

'Good morning, Sheriff. And I'm well rested from my travels.'

He laughed aloud. 'I was about to take coffee in the hotel,' he said.

'And so was I,' she said. 'Would you care to join me?'

'Yes, ma'am. Anyways, I needed to speak with you.'

Her fine eyebrows lifted a fraction. 'Then I'm glad we met, Mr Harding.'

Five minutes later they were seated at a small table in the corner of one of the hotel's four parlours. In front of them were cups and saucers and a large metal coffee pot. The young woman, who was obviously known to Amy, had poured their coffee before leaving them alone, making sure that the door to the parlour was left ajar.

'Emma is one of our successes,' Amy said, referring to the maid. 'If we hadn't taken her under our wing she'd have been working in the Silver Lode. We have a Ladies' Society in Jackson,' she explained. 'We try to do our best for the poorer citizens of the town.' She took a small sip of her coffee. 'You said you wanted to speak with me.'

'I'm beginning to think again about the death of the Englishman. Maybe it wasn't an accident.'

Her eyes widened with pleasure and for a moment Harding thought that to prompt that look in his direction was worth him saying he'd think about anything again, even that the moon was made of cheese.

'Last night you doubted me so much.'

'I hadn't heard of Josh Wake last night.'

'But I'm not sure if the two men ever met.'

'I'll be straight with you, Miss Dawson. I don't know yet if there is a connection. Dale died two weeks ago; Wake was attacked two weeks ago.' Harding leaned forward. 'Miss Dawson, I don't believe in happenstance. There's a chance that something's going on we know nothing about. Have

39

Dale's boxes been put on the stage?'

Amy shook her head. 'They'll not be going for a couple of months.'

'I want you to search them for anything unusual, anything that might give us some notion of why someone would wish to kill him.'

'Very well. I can do that.'

'Who is Mr Wake's clerk? I need to speak with him.'

Amy shook her head. 'Tom Jenkins, but I happen to know he's in Cheyenne. He'll return on the stage next week.' She looked at the tiny watch pinned to her jacket. 'Now you must excuse me, or the ladies of the town will wonder why I'm late.'

Harding stood up, and watched Amy walk from the room. For the first time he realized that his time spent in Canada and out West was falling from his speech when he spoke with her.

'You'll be talkin' like a Pennsylvania lawyer afore you leave Jackson,' he said to the empty room. Then he laughed aloud.

'That's a darned good day's work, Charlie Wilson.' Harding looked up from his desk. 'Light a coupla lamps so I can count all this money.'

Charlie jumped to his feet suddenly, causing Bruno to lift his head, his tongue lolling from his wide mouth.

'You have any trouble?'

'The blacksmith Schmidt was ornery, tol' me he'd pay come the fall. I tol' him he could refuse to pay now, and we'd be back tomorrow to throw him in jail. Mrs Schmidt gave him hell. Or I reckon she did. She was screamin' at him in German.' Charlie grinned. 'He paid up.'

'Mayor Bannon's gonna be mighty pleased.'

Ten minutes later Harding was locking up a pile of money

into the strongbox set in the stucco wall back of the pot-bellied stove. 'OK, Charlie, we start our rounds tonight. From now on 'bout this time we're both gonna take a stroll 'round town, an' make sure everythin's quiet.'

Charlie put down his coffee and stood up, settling his new Colt on his hip. 'OK, ready to go.'

'No, you ain't.' Harding took a key from the drawer of his desk, and walked across to the gun-rack, bolted to the wall. 'We do our rounds with these.' He took down two scatter-guns and relocked the gun-rack. He handed one of the weapons to Charlie.

Patches of light were thrown from one or two stores on to the hardpack of Main Street when the two men ventured outside. Harding guessed that a couple of the storekeepers were working late. Together, Harding and Wilson crossed Main Street and entered the Silver Lode, looking around for a few moments. But the place was quiet and there was no sign of Pierce or any of his men. One of the calico queens offered Charlie a free one as they turned to leave and his face was red as the two men pushed through the batwing doors back on to the boardwalk.

'Sorry to spoil your night, Deputy,' said Harding laconi-cally.

'Aw, she was just joshin' me.'

Harding resisted the temptation to keep on at his deputy and set his face. 'OK, you take this side, an' I'll walk the other side. Keep level with me. When we get to the end we'll turn 'round and walk back here. Keep your scatter-gun ready like this.' Harding held his own scatter-gun, angled a few inches away from his chest. 'Makes it faster to fire.'

Satisfied with Charlie's nod that he understood, Harding turned and crossed Main Street. He stepped up to the boardwalk and held up a hand to signal his deputy. At a steady pace they began their patrol of the town. There were few people around. Once night had settled, the townsfolk tended to stay in their homes.

While checking the doors of closed stores, Harding thought for a few moments about the absence of Pierce and his men. Were they out of town up to no good or was there a simple explanation? After all, it was early and maybe Pierce and his wife, Beth, were upstairs in their own rooms.

He looked across and saw that Charlie had taken his cue from Harding and was checking the doors of the darkened stores. His deputy was turning out to be a good man. Maybe by the fall, if Pierce had gone from the town, Charlie might make sheriff. At least he'd have a good chance if he stood for election.

A woman's loud scream cut through his thoughts. Ten yards ahead, a woman burst out of the alley alongside the livery. Despite her long skirts she managed to jump up steps and scuttle along the boardwalk in the direction of the dry goods store. Harding broke into a run.

'It's OK, ma'am! Sheriff Harding here. You're safe now.'

The woman, sobbing loudly, turned to face him as he caught up with her.

'I was takin' Mr Fielding his supper,' she spluttered. 'A man grabbed me, and started to—' Her voice trailed away, and she began to weep again.

'Charlie!' Harding called across the street. 'Over here.' He turned back to the woman. 'I guess you're Mrs Fielding,'

The woman, her apron pulled up over her face, nodded vigorously. He could just make out what she was saying. 'I was taking Mr Fielding his supper 'cos he's working late on his books.'

Harding turned to his deputy who had joined him. 'See Mrs Fielding to the store, and stay on this side of the street. The no-good must be somewhere between this alley and the livery. Make sure he doesn't make a break 'cross the street.'

Charlie nodded and held out his arm to Mrs Fielding who was beginning to regain her composure, her apron dropped to cover her skirts. 'Take my arm, ma'am, an' we'll soon have you with your husband.'

Harding loosened the butt of his Colt, his scatter-gun held in his free hand. He didn't think it would come to a gunfight but he wasn't taking any chances. He watched his deputy and Mrs Fielding take a few paces along the board-walk and, satisfied, jumped down to the hardpack leading to the alley. Warily, he began to move to the dark area behind the building. Only the stars and the half-moon threw any light.

Nothing moved in the alley. Keeping close against the wooden timbers he worked his way around the corner of the building. The no-good had to be between him and the alley-way beyond the dry goods store. If Charlie spotted him he'd yell. He took another ten cautious paces. There! Something glinted. Maybe the buckle on a belt.

'Hold it right there! Sheriff Harding here!'

Nothing moved in the shadows and Harding's muscles tightened. This was no drunken cowboy or stupid young townsman. He was up against some no-good who knew what he was about. Without hesitating he raised his scatter-gun and fired off a shell at a height he knew would be above the man in the shadows.

There was a startled curse and the man stepped forward. Harding had an instant to realize the man was reaching for his gun. With one smooth move, the result of many hours of practice, he drew his Colt and shot the man in the foot.

The shadows erupted with a screamed curse and a figure pitched forward and fell, still cursing, face down on to the hardpack. Harding stepped forward and pulled the man's gun from its holster. With the toe of his boot he turned the man over.

'Well, howdy, Frenchie. Mebbe you should've tried a bribe.'

'You've shot me in my goddamned foot, you sonovabitch!'

Harding looked up as Charlie came rushing along the building towards them.

'C'mon an' give me a hand, Charlie.' Harding called. 'Ol' Frenchie needs a hand to the jailhouse. He ain't walkin' too good.'

Ten minutes later Frenchie was in a chair in front of Harding's desk, emptying his pockets. Harding finished writing and looked up. 'OK, stand up.'

'I cain't, an' you know it.'

'Doc Radman will be along to see to the two slugs in your foot.'

Frenchie glared at him. 'One,' he snarled.

'By the time Doc Radman's here there'll be two if you don't stand.'

'Fer cris'sakes, you cain't do this!' Frenchie glared across the desk, and then realizing that Harding might carry out his threat, struggled to his feet, cursing as he did so.

'OK Charlie. Search him.'

The deputy half-turned Frenchie and thoroughly felt down the whole length of his body. Satisfied, he stood back. 'OK, he's clear.'

Harding's mouth twisted. 'Turn him around, and do the same.'

The deputy did as he was told. 'What in tarnation you got here, Frenchie?' From the top of Frenchie's pants Charlie pulled a long vicious-looking knife encased in a leather sheath.

'Bet you can hit a bull's eye at twenty paces with that,' said Harding drily. 'OK, Frenchie, you'll get three a day, an' Seb Haines'll take you out to the privy in the yard. Seb doesn't carry a gun. You try an' escape from Seb, an' you're not gonna go far with that foot o' yourn. That'll give us a reason to shoot you down an' save the town's money keepin' you until the judge gets here.' He stared hard at Frenchie. 'You got all that?'

'I got it.'

Harding nodded at Charlie. 'Throw him in the cage,' he said, 'an' let Seb know he'll be on jail duty from tomorrow.' He picked up his pen, and turned another page of his journal.

CHAPTER FIVE

Harding was eating his breakfast in the Chinaman's place when he was aware of a shadow above him. He looked up, expecting to see Lee Ming, who worked the tables, holding a fresh pot of coffee. Instead, the stylishly dressed figure of Jake Pierce, coffee in hand, stood a few feet from his table.

'You mind if I join you? We've matters to talk on.'

Harding pushed away his plate, looking around for more coffee and holding out his cup for the young boy to fill it from the metal pot.

'And what matters we got to talk about, Mr Pierce?'

He turned back and nodded towards the chair on the other side of the table, indicating that Pierce should take a seat. The saloon owner eased himself into the chair.

'You're holding one of my men. I need him.'

'The judge will be here next month. Frenchie's staying where he is until he gets taken to Cheyenne. I warned you all the first day I was in town.'

Pierce's mouth set in a hard line. 'For cris'sakes, Harding! I've been to see Fielding and offered him money.' Pierce let out a bitter laugh. 'Damned fool said he wants justice not money.' He leaned forward, glaring at Harding. 'You talk to

Fielding. I'll be generous to his wife, and I'll pay any fine you care to set.'

Harding leaned back. 'You ain't livin' in the forties, Pierce. Wyoming will be a state of the Union one day when the rule of law is taken for normal. The day's over when you can buy your way out of trouble. Now get away from my table and let me have my second coffee in peace.'

Ashen-faced, Pierce got up from his chair. 'You've just made the mistake of your life, Harding,' he said, his voice trembling with rage. 'You'll never leave this town alive.'

He turned on his heel and, brushing aside Lee Ming who stood in his path, stormed out of the chop-house.

Harding was still digesting the large steak he'd eaten for breakfast at the Chinaman's when Charlie Wilson turned away from the window overlooking Main Street, a thoughtful expression on his face.

'Stagecoach just drove in, Sheriff. Tom Jenkins, Mr Wake's clerk, should be back in town.'

'I wanna talk to him. Let's go take a look.'

'C'mon, Bruno,' Charlie ordered. Obediently the dog struggled to his feet and followed his master towards the door.

'Mebbe we should put a badge on Bruno's collar,' Harding said.

Charlie whirled around, a broad smile on his face. 'That's a great notion, Sheriff—' He broke off, his face reddening as he saw the broad grin on Harding's face. 'Aw, heck,' he muttered. 'I knew all the time you was just joshing me.'

Together, accompanied by Bruno, the two lawmen crossed Main Street, heading for the stage office, touching their hats to acknowledge the greetings from the townsfolk.

'It feels mighty good for folks to greet me like they do. But I guess it's only the badge,' Charlie said.

'They know you've the courage to pin it on your shirt, Charlie.' He pointed to the young man getting down from the stage. 'Is that Tom Jenkins?'

'Yeah, that's him.'

'Mr Jenkins, a word with you,' Harding called out.

The young man turned at the sound of his name. He called something to the driver about his boxes, and then moved along the boardwalk to the two lawmen.

'Guess you're the new sheriff from Cheyenne I heard about,' he said. 'What can I do for you?'

'Mr Wake's in a bad way. I can't ask him questions but you might help.'

'Anything, if it means you catch up with the no-goods.'

'D'you know if Mr Wake and the Englishman Robert Dale ever met?'

Jenkins didn't hesitate. 'Sure they did. Day before Mr Dale had his riding accident he came to see Mr Wake. They had a long conversation.'

'Do you know what about?'

The lawyer's clerk shook his head. 'No, but they both went out riding together the following day. Somewhere around the homesteads, if I remember right.' His mouth tightened. 'It was a bad day for both of them.'

Harding nodded. 'You're right, Mr Jenkins.' He held out his hand to the young man. 'But I'm obliged to you for your help.'

He was turning away to speak with Charlie when he stopped suddenly, staring back at the stagecoach as a tall, powerfully built man in range clothes stepped down from the stage.

'Frank Warden!' Harding called. 'What in tarnation are you doin' in Jackson?'

The tall man strode towards the two lawmen, his face wreathed in smiles.

'Howdy, Clay. I'm here to see you, but first I need to wash up and get a change of clothes. Sooner the railroad company puts in a few spur lines the happier I'm gonna be. I feel as if I've darned well walked from Cheyenne.' He looked down at Bruno. 'Heck, that's some dog.'

Harding waved a hand. 'Frank, this here smart feller is Charlie Wilson, my deputy. Charlie, this is Mr Frank Warden who has saved my life a coupla times.'

'Only cos I like playin' cards with you.' Warden winked at Charlie. 'Take my tip, Deputy. You're ever short of cash, play cards with Mr Harding. His brain stops working when he sees a deck of cards.'

'I'll keep that in mind, sir.'

'OK, Clay.' Warden said briskly, 'I'll see you in an hour. I guess you'll be in your office.'

'You can tell me what's happening in Cheyenne.'

'Plenty, but leave it for now.'

As the two lawmen walked back to the office, Harding could see that Charlie was bursting with unasked questions. They were back in their office, having taken coffee from the pot on the stove, and were seated behind their desks before Harding gave his deputy the go-ahead.

'OK, Charlie, fire away with your questions.'

Charlie's mouth twitched. 'Yeah, there are a coupla things I ain't got straight in my mind. You told me about what Mr Wake was able to say to you. An' that made no sense. If there was gold in these parts some miner would have found it long ago. Then you seem to reckon that Mr Wake and the Englishmen are connected.' Charlie shrugged. 'I ain't sure what you're thinkin', that's all.'

'OK, just s'pose there is gold around here, an' I ain't sayin' there is, but the Englishman has spent weeks searching the area around the homesteads for rocks. Just s'pose he had found gold. He ain't gonna come rushin' into town shoutin' about it. But he might just want to talk with a lawyer.'

Charlie looked thoughtful. 'Or maybe Old Zack found gold and asked the Englishman for help with the lawyer.'

'Who the hell's Old Zack?'

'He's an old man who's got a cabin out by the river. He useta talk with the Englishman, help him collect his rocks and get paid in whiskey.'

'If gold is there it don't really matter who found it. Dale came to see Josh Wake and the following day they ride out together to the homesteads.'

'Or mebbe they were lookin' 'round the abandoned coal tunnels. Mebbe the Fremont expedition found coal but missed gold.' Charlie slapped his forehead with his open hand. 'Fer crissakes! That's why Pierce is gettin' so ornery about us holdin' Frenchie!'

'I ain't followin' you.'

'Afore he took to the owlhoot trail, Frenchie was a miner. If there is gold in one of those tunnels and Pierce has had a sniff of it, he'd need a miner.'

'Pierce would need more than someone who'd spent his days pannin' for gold or scratchin' at a diggin'.'

'Frenchie was a real miner. Worked the coal back East in lotsa places.'

'So why's he ended up with a no-good like Pierce?'

'He couldn't work. He slugged his boss when he reckoned what he was told to do was dangerous. No mine would take him on after that.'

'OK, that makes sense, but Pierce could bring in a miner from some place.'

Charlie shook his head. 'Not from 'round these parts. There ain't been miners here for thirty years. Anyways, a miner ain't gonna leave his diggin's or a safe job for some story about gold.'

Harding frowned. 'You sure about Frenchie?'

Charlie nodded vigorously. 'That Texan gal in the Lode. The one who was joshin' me the night we put Frenchie in the cage. She told me.'

For a few moments Harding looked across to his deputy. 'You carry on like this, Charlie, and the Pinkertons will be after hiring you,' he said. 'But remember, we're doin' a lot of guessin' here. Mebbe Doc Radman had it right. With a bad head wound, Wake could say anythin'.'

He looked to the door as it was pushed open and Hector Housman stepped in from the boardwalk. His fleshy face showed a broad smile, a gold tooth glinting at the corner of his mouth.

'Good day, Mr Harding,' he said loudly. He looked over at Charlie, his eyes lingering on the badge pinned to Charlie's vest. 'Good to see that badge on you, Charlie. Your gran'pappy must be real proud of you.'

'He is, Mr Housman. An' I owe it to him an' Mr Harding.'

'What can we do for you, Mr Housman?'

'It's what I can do for you, Sheriff.'

'Then take a seat. Always a pleasure to hear a man talkin' that way.'

'The best week I've had with the paper these last seven years. The folks couldn't get enough of your account of meeting Lotta Crabtree.' Housman waved his hand in the air with a flourish. 'An' I can return the favour. I've found something about gold or mebbe I should say the school-marm found it.'

'That's mighty interesting. Was there a mine or somethin' in these parts?'

'Nothin' like that. There's never been a notion that gold could be here. But in '69, afore my time, the paper carried an anniversary article about a gold robbery fifty miles west of here. Ten years afore, in '59, a wagon carrying Army gold

51

headin' for Fort Laramie was stolen by the very men who were meant to protect it. The sergeant and three troopers killed an officer and the wagon driver and then made off with the gold.'

'Well, I'll be damned! I've been around Cheyenne for a time. Nobody's ever talked about that.'

Housman shrugged. 'It all happened a long time ago. People forget.'

'Did the Army catch up with the thieves?'

'They caught up with the sergeant and two of the troopers, and strung 'em up. The youngest trooper, a young feller name of Isaac Holt, made his escape. Some thought the Shoshone had given him shelter but nothing was ever proved.'

'When did the schoolmarm find this?'

'Mebbe an hour ago.'

Harding swung around in his chair. 'Charlie, you get after the schoolmarm. Tell her if she breathes a word about this to anyone I'll have her picking hemp down in Cheyenne. And here,' he thrust his hand into his vest pocket, and pulled out several bills. 'Give her five dollars an' tell her she's done great work.'

'C'mon Bruno. Let's hit the trail.'

'That's mighty generous of you, Sheriff,' Housman said, after Charlie had left. 'After all, it's yesterday's news.'

'I want you to give me your word you'll not say anythin' to anyone about this.'

'Sure, like I said—'

'I want your word, Mr Housman,' Harding cut in.

For a moment Housman looked startled, and then he nodded. 'You have my word.'

'Does your printer know about this?'

Housman shook his head. 'William's at home today.'

As Housman finished speaking, Charlie opened the door.

'I was lucky. The schoolmarm was heading for Mr Fielding's store. She understands, an' she's real grateful for the money. An' Mr Warden's on his way over to see you.'

Housman stood up. 'Then I'll be on my way. Good day to you, Sheriff.'

Through the open door Harding saw Frank Warden step aside to allow Housman to pass. Harding waited until Warden had entered the office and taken the seat in front of his desk. Warden hadn't said a word, and Harding wondered why his friend was so quiet.

'You gonna tell me why you're here?'

Warden hesitated. 'I ain't sure how you're gonna take this, Clay.'

'Why don't you just tell me, an' we'll see?'

'Governor Thayer wants you back in Cheyenne. You're to return there immediately, an' I'm to take your place as sheriff of Jackson Creek.'

For several seconds there was silence in the office. Then Harding spoke.

'That's damned crazy, Frank. I ain't leavin'. Anyways, I thought you were sortin' out that trouble down south of the Territory.'

Warden breathed in deeply. 'Clay, the governor sent me because I'm your senior in rank.'

Harding's mouth twitched. 'Yeah, by three months.'

'But that's enough to give a lawful order, Major. You're to return to Cheyenne, this very day.'

'Hold on,' exploded Charlie. 'What the hell's goin' on here? An' why talk like that, calling the sheriff a major?'

Warden looked at Harding. 'Can we trust him?'

'Sure.'

Warden turned to Charlie. 'We're a team of four Army officers assigned to Governor Thayer for special duties. We handle business like the lawlessness seen in this town.'

'If you're Army why aren't you in uniform?' Charlie protested.

'It's against the law for the Army to interfere in civilian matters,' Harding said. 'Our commissions are suspended for the three years we serve the governor.'

Charlie's face was red with anger. 'But you ain't gonna just ride outa town.'

'I have to,' Harding said. 'I have to obey orders.'

'But that's goddamned crazy! An' how about what the schoolmarm found?'

'Somethin' I should know about?' Warden asked.

'She found a newspaper report on Army gold stolen thirty years ago.'

Warden made a mouth. 'It's today I'm concerned with. You'd better brief me on what's goin' on in the town afore you leave.'

Charlie stood up. 'I ain't gonna sit here and listen to this,' he said hotly. 'I'm gonna take a walk about town.' He touched his dog's head. 'C'mon, Bruno. You an' me ain't gonna walk out on the good folks of Jackson.'

'He's ornery about this,' Warden said, when the two men were alone.

'He'll settle. Charlie's a good man, an' I'd be obliged if you taught him as much as you know while you're here.'

'Sure, Clay. Now let's get to that briefin'.'

For the next hour Harding described what had happened since he'd left Cheyenne. Warden raised his eyebrows when Harding told him about the attempt on his life before he'd even reached the town. Once or twice Harding referred to his journal about separate incidents and explained why Frenchie was being held for the judge, and that Mrs Fielding was ready to give evidence. He outlined the routine for the prisoner and the duties of Seb Haines around the jailhouse. He mentioned the gold but again Warden dismissed the notion that the gold, if it even existed around Jackson, could ever be found after so much time had passed.

'Charlie can arrange my boxes to be sent on,' Harding said. 'I'll ride south from here and pick up the railroad.'

'I guess you've made your mark here, Clay. You reckon the townsfolk gonna support me after you've gone?'

'They're just glad they've got a sheriff. Pierce was rollin' over 'em for a time.' Harding stood up. 'But watch him, Frank, he's as dangerous as a diamondback. Charlie will take you to the mayor; he'll set easy with the changeover. The clapboard next door is yourn, A young gal name o' Lucy, Charlie's sister, looks after it. She's as sassy as hell but I've been givin' her twenty dollars a month an' she's worth every cent.' Harding held out his hand to Warden who shook it vigorously.

'I'll pick up a coupla bits and pieces an' be on my way.' Harding forced a smile. 'Take care o' Jackson for me. I'll see you in Cheyenne come the fall.' He picked up his journal and, touching the brim of his hat with one finger, he left the office to make his way to the General Store. A sudden thought came to him as he was passing the hotel and he turned to enter through the wide doorway. Behind the desk the elderly clerk looked up from his books and greeted him.

'Howdy, Sheriff. What can I do for you?'

'The Ladies' Society, I think they call themselves,' he began.

'That's the name, Mr Harding. They're meeting now in the big parlour.'

Harding breathed in deeply. 'Could you go and tell Miss Dawson I need to speak with her. Tell her it's important.'

'Sure, Sheriff. You can see her in the little parlour where you took coffee the other day.'

55

Harding walked along the hallway and stepped into the small parlour. There was no one else present and he was thankful that he would have Amy alone when he told her he was leaving Jackson. A couple of minutes later she came into the room a concerned expression on her face.

'Is something wrong, Mr Harding?'

'Let's sit down. I've something to tell you.' He waited until she had settled her skirts before he took a deep breath. 'I'm quitting Jackson, and returning to Cheyenne.' He hadn't intended to be so blunt, but he could think of no other way of giving her the news. 'I could be away some time.'

'But why—?' Her voice trailed away, confusion showing in her eyes.

'Orders from the governor. I work for him, and he wants me back in Cheyenne.'

'But you can't just leave us. I'm sure Mr Wilson will do his best but he's no match for that devil Pierce.'

'I'm not leaving him alone to face Pierce. A good friend of mine, Frank Warden, is taking my place.'

She turned her head an inch or two, looking away from Harding. 'But I don't want you to go.' She looked at him again across the low table, her face pink. 'There! I've said it. You must think me quite a hussy.'

Harding leaned forwards to close the space between them. 'I swear I'll be back.' He smiled and reached out to take her hand. 'And I pray you'll be waiting for me. Now I want you to do something for me. Can you delay sending back Robert Dale's effects?'

She nodded. 'Yes, they're going back to England later but his family aren't expecting them for a while.'

'Have you searched them as I asked?'

'I've opened the first box but it holds only clothes.'

'OK, keep looking. Now I'm going to tell you something

you must keep to yourself. You're not even to tell your mother. Do you understand?'

Amy's lips pressed together. 'Yes,' she said. 'I understand.'

'Army gold was stolen about thirty years ago by renegade soldiers not far from Jackson. It's possible they hid the gold close to the town, maybe inside one of the mining tunnels around the homesteads.'

'But it would take years to search the tunnels,' Amy said.

'I agree, but I'm guessing that your Englishman found something which gave a clue to its whereabouts, and that's why he was killed. Say nothing and when I return we'll continue looking.'

'But Mr Dale's death must mean someone else is looking for the gold.' Her eyes widened, and she breathed in. 'Pierce,' she said.

Harding looked at her for a moment. 'Yes,' he said. 'But if the gold is around Jackson it's been here for thirty years. We have to hope that it stays hidden until I get back.'

She looked at him for several seconds as if she were summoning the courage to say something. Finally she spoke.

'I could come with you to Cheyenne.'

Surprise must have registered on his face, and involuntarily he squeezed her hand. For a moment Harding was tempted to accept her offer; he had more than enough money for both of them. But Amy would never be received by any of the families in Cheyenne who would view her as a mere concubine of one of the governor's men. On their return the ladies of the town would snub her as being no better than one of the girls in the Silver Lode. He placed his free hand over hers.

'Nothing would give me greater pleasure, but the governor could send me anywhere he chooses. Stay with your mother until I return.'

He stood up. 'Goodbye, Amy,' he said, using her given

name for the first time, 'I hope to be back soon.' He gave a brief bow, and left her sitting in the parlour staring straight ahead.

CHAPTER SIX

He made good time on the trail heading south but by late afternoon Harding decided to quit for the day. He reckoned he'd make the railroad in two days, and there was no sense in pushing his roan. Lose his mount in this part of the country, and he could be in real trouble.

Over to the east, maybe less than a mile away, was a lake. If it had a name it hadn't been marked on the rough map he'd found in the bottom drawer of his desk back in the sheriff's office. He walked the roan across the bunch and buffalo grass, his thoughts occupied with what had happened since his arrival in Jackson Creek.

After the job the governor needed him for, he'd be high-tailing it back to the town. Amy Dawson would be waiting for him, of that he was sure. Maybe it was time to quit the Army. He could take Amy back East and restart his law practice. Although how he'd settle to a life behind a desk and wearing a city suit he was no longer sure. He'd had the opportunity when he finished with the North West Mounted Police but instead had opted to join Frank Warden in Cheyenne.

Warden would look after Charlie. He was able to take care of himself, and was a good man, even if, Harding thought wryly, he was sharp with a deck of cards. Frank wouldn't remain in Jackson longer than a few months and that would give Charlie his chance. That's if Pierce didn't outwit them both. Some days it was tempting to look back to the days when the strict rule of law wasn't enforced, and it was enough for a sheriff to know that some men should be dangling at the end of a rope.

He reached the edge of the lake, moving into a small stand of cottonwoods which would provide good shelter for the night. He swung easily from the saddle, and unbuckled the rig from his roan. Pulling out of his saddle-bag a couple of old saddle-ties, he dropped on one knee to hobble the roan. The animal was unlikely to stray but he was taking no chances. Hobbled, the horse would be free to move with no risk of taking to the hills.

From his saddle-bag he took the hook and length of line he'd bought at the General Store in Jackson Creek, and then, carrying his throwing knife, taken from where it hung from the cord at the nape of his neck, he looked around at the trees. He found the low branches thicker than he'd first thought and he slid the knife back into its sheath and pulled out his broad-bladed knife from the top of his boot. Then he walked among the trees until he found a suitable straight branch and cut it to serve as a fish-pole.

His luck was in, and twenty minutes later a couple of fish were sizzling in his mess-pan over a blazing fire. The good smell helped to fight off his feeling of gloom at having to leave Jackson Creek. He reckoned Frank was an able man, but back in Cheyenne he couldn't avoid noticing that maybe Frank had lost that sharpness he'd showed a few years back. He swore under his breath. It rankled that his own departure could have Pierce thinking he'd gained some sort of victory.

'Nothing I can do now,' he said aloud.

At the sound of his voice the roan raised its head, although whether in agreement or not with the spoken words, Harding couldn't decide. An hour later, after finishing his coffee, he was sound asleep, his head on his saddle and his blanket pulled up to his nose against the chills of the Wyoming spring night.

He was back on the trail an hour after sunup. The early morning light twinkled on the dew which covered the grass either side of the trail. At one time the trail must have been heavily used as the ground was beaten down and the bunch and buffalo grass was taking its time in recovering. He turned in his saddle to push his hand down to the bottom of his saddle-bag, remembering the candy he'd bought before he'd left Jackson.

'Just get me through—' he said aloud, and then broke off as he stared at the higher ground maybe a mile or so back along the trail. A rider was heading towards him at a gallop. Behind his mount were two more horses which Harding guessed were tethered to the rider's saddle. Feller must be in a damned hurry. Maybe he was concerned that he'd miss the train that went through to Cheyenne.

Harding sat easily in his saddle, watching the rider approach. A hundred yards away the rider was close enough for Harding to recognize his features.

'You're in one hell of a hurry, Matt Parkes,' he called.

With a shout of greeting, the liveryman from Jackson slowed his three horses and reined in alongside Harding.

'You sure make a man ride hard, Sheriff.'

'I ain't the sheriff no more. Why you been chasin' me?'

'Four of Pierce's men attacked the jailhouse a coupla hours after you left, tryin' to break out Frenchie.'

Harding's muscles tightened. 'An' did Sheriff Warden see them off?'

'All four were shot down, Mr Harding. But the new sheriff is dead.'

Harding felt the blood drain from his face with shock. Frank Warden, his fellow lieutenant back during the War, and both of them had survived without a scratch; later, after he'd quit the law, he and Frank working together up north, surviving hell knows what, and then for Frank to lose his life in a small town like Jackson Creek. What damnable irony.

'And Charlie Wilson?'

'Charlie took a slug in his arm but Doc Badman patched him up. He's sitting in the office, a coupla scatter-guns on his desk, his pistol on his knee.' Parkes eased himself in his saddle. 'Charlie wants you back, Mr Harding. The decent folk in town want you back, or that sonovabitch Pierce an' his no-goods are gonna ride right over us.'

Harding thought for a moment. 'I'm gonna ride back aways for a few minutes. Give you a chance to settle yourself, now you've found me.'

Parkes nodded. 'OK, Mr Harding.'

Harding turned the head of his mount allowing the animal to walk back along the trail. He needed time to think away from Parkes's gaze. His orders were to return to Cheyenne immediately, but had Frank Warden's death changed everything? He couldn't claim later that he hadn't been given a lawful order. Sure, he could put together some story of being out of Jackson for a day or so, and never actually seeing Frank. But that meant lying to his superiors in Cheyenne, and he knew he couldn't do that.

There was one possible chance, he realized. Warden's death did make a difference. Cheyenne wanted to see the rule of law in Jackson Creek. If he could rid the town of Pierce and also find the stolen Army gold then any talk of his disobeying a lawful order would be quelled. But what if there was no gold to find? And supposing he was forced to ask for reinforcements from Cheyenne to bring law back to the town?

He was taking a big gamble. If he lost, it would probably mean a court martial. He'd be booted out of the Army, and there'd be no chance then of going back to practice law. He had no proof that the renegades had hidden the gold around Jackson. He had only a hunch. His life, he knew was at a divided trail.

'Aw, to hell with it,' he said aloud. 'If the gold is there, and I find it, they'll probably make me a colonel.'

He turned his roan to ride back to Parkes. 'Come noon I'm gonna need one of your mounts. We'll make Jackson by tomorrow after sunup.'

The sun had been up two or three hours when Harding and Parkes came off the trail to reach the hardpack of Jackson's Main Street. The townsfolk who were about their business stopped to watch the two riders rein in outside the sheriff's office.

'Good to see you back, Sheriff,' someone called out, and there was a burst of applause from along the boardwalk.

'Tol' you folks wanted you back,' Parkes said. 'I'll take your mount down to the livery. The animal will need a good feedin' after these last coupla days.'

'I'm obliged to you,' Harding said, as he stepped down from the saddle, feeling the stiffness in his legs. He took down his saddle-bag and went up the steps to the boardwalk. The door to the office was open a few inches.

'You ain't sleepin' there, Charlie Wilson?'

Startled, the deputy sat up straight, his face pale with exhaustion, dark shadows showing beneath his eyes. High up on his arm, something bulged beneath his shirt, and Harding guessed that was where his deputy had taken a slug. On the desk before Wilson were two-scatter guns and a Winchester long gun. The top drawer of the desk had been turned upside down and half pushed back. On the solid top

63

sat Charlie's Colt.

'They tried to break out Frenchie, Mr Harding—'

Harding held up a hand. 'Parkes tol' me. How did Frank Warden die?'

'The four no-goods were in the dirt on the street, all dead, we thought. Mr Warden went out to take a look. One of 'em was wounded an' layin' doggo. As Mr Warden stepped down to the street, the no-good rolled over an' shot him.'

'Is the no-good still alive?'

Charlie shook his head. 'I killed the sonovabitch.'

Harding nodded. Maybe the dead man could have lived long enough to tell who had given him orders. He walked over to the pot-bellied stove and poured coffee into a tin mug.

'OK, Charlie. We go on as before. We're gonna see Pierce hang, for he's behind all this. I've had time to think while ridin' south an' I reckon those renegade soldiers hid the gold some place 'round these parts. We're gonna go after it.'

'So what we gonna do now? Throw Pierce in jail?'

'We try that an' he'll claim that he fired those four no-goods a week ago, an' they were tryin' to break out their partner afore they left town. A judge would be mighty ornery I called on him. We'll get Pierce, an' we'll make sure we've got enough to hang him. Anyways, you ain't gonna do anythin'. You're goin' back to your gran'pappy an' get some sleep.'

'I ain't tired!' Charlie protested. 'How about you? You bin ridin' the trail the last coupla days.'

Harding's mouth twitched. 'I've done this before, lotsa times. You're goin' to your bunk, an' that's an order.'

With a deep sigh Charlie got up from behind the desk. He took the scatter-guns and the Winchester to the gun-rack and secured them. 'Seb's gonna come in at noon, an' give

Frenchie some food. I'll be back as soon as I can.' He waited at the door until Bruno was beside his leg and then looked across at Harding. 'I'm damned pleased you're back,' he said, and closed the door.

Alone, Harding pulled his journal from his saddle-bag. One day soon he might have to give an account of events in Jackson. Whether his journal would help to plead his case at a court martial or to account for his success at finding the Army's gold only time would tell. But, on reflection, maybe he'd ignore his journal until the following day. Before he took up his pen there was something he must do.

He left the office and walked across Main Street, acknowledging the warm greetings of the townsfolk. Somebody from the Lode must have spotted him for there was a flurry of activity outside the saloon and a man rose from his chair and hurried through the batwing doors. Harding entered the hotel to find a different clerk, this one much younger than the one he'd spoken with previously.

'Does the Ladies' Society meet today?' Harding asked.

'They meet most days,' the young man said. He glanced at the star on Harding's vest. 'We're glad you're back in Jackson, sir.'

'Thanks. Is the small parlour empty?'

'Yes, it is. I guess you wish to see Miss Dawson.'

'Heck! No secrets in Jackson!'

'Not one, Mr Harding.' The clerk smiled. 'Miss Dawson will be along.'

'Just tell her the sheriff wishes to have a word. Don't mention my name.'

Harding walked along the hall to the small parlour and stood looking across the street towards the saloon. Three men, their heads bent to each other, were deep in conversation. He didn't have to guess what they were talking about. He'd been waiting only a couple of minutes when he heard movement behind him, and he turned to face the door.

'Oh, my God! You really are back!' Amy shrieked with delight, and ran across the room to throw her arms around his neck. 'People told me they'd seen you, but I thought they were mistaken.'

He smiled down at her upturned face wreathed in smiles. 'The ladies of the society see you like this, and we'll both have to leave town.'

She pressed her head against his chest. 'I don't care! You're here, that's all that matters.' She pulled away, her head back, looking up at him. 'Have you been sent back here because Mr Warden was killed?'

'Something like that,' he said. 'I'll make Pierce pay for Frank's death, take my word.'

'I did what you said and searched more of Mr Dale's boxes, and I've already found something odd,' she said. 'It's a badge of some sort. I think it could have something to do with the Army. I can't understand how Robert Dale would have something like that. Come to the house tomorrow, and I'll show it to you.'

'I'll do that. Now, you'd better go back to the ladies.'

'I couldn't understand while they were all giggling like silly schoolgirls.' She paused to look back at him as she reached the doorway. 'Clay, I'm so glad you're back.'

He smiled and waved her on. To hell with Cheyenne and orders! He was just glad to be back in Jackson Creek.

CHAPTER SEVEN

An hour or so after the sun was up Harding sat at his desk writing in his journal, describing the events of the previous day. Regardless of what he would eventually have to face in Cheyenne his boss would require his words so as to fill in his own journal. Zacharias Hogg, whose closest friends used his full name and never addressed him as 'Zack', could be ornery if details were not on paper.

Harding put down his pen and sat staring across the office. He'd suddenly remembered the name of the old-timer who helped the Englishman collect his rocks. Charlie had mentioned him, he recalled. Had he, Harding, missed something there? There was a chance that Old Zack could shed some light on what the Englishman had been about. Maybe he knew why Dale and the lawyer, Josh Wake, had been riding out together. He'd need to ask Radman if Wake was able to answer more questions.

He picked up his pen again, signed his journal entry and appended the date. The old railroad clock that had found its way to Jackson and was now pinned to the stucco wall showed he had another hour before he rode out to see Amy Dawson. The thought of seeing her again brought a smile to his face. He hoped she'd found something useful.

The street door opened and he looked up, expecting to

see Charlie who he'd sent off to chase up some brat who was playing hooky from school. Instead, he was surprised to see Beth Pierce.

'Good mornin', Mrs Pierce. What brings you here so early in the morning?'

'I need you to do somethin' for me, Mr Harding.'

'Take a seat an' tell me what it is.' He waited while she settled her skirts. 'So, fire away.'

'I want you to come to the Lode and speak with my husband.'

'If Pierce wishes to talk he can walk across here.' Harding breathed in deeply. 'You take my advice, you'll get far away from that man. I heard he was trouble back in Pittsburgh an' he's trouble in the West. He's gonna hang one of these days, and you don't want any part of him.'

Beth Pierce's face grew older. 'How simple you make it sound, Mr Harding, with your fancy education and fine kinfolk! Where would I go? I'd end up in another saloon in some godforsaken place being pawed by drunken cowboys an' worse. The young men would make fun of me, and the old men would have their hands inside my dress hopin' to bed me for a coupla dollars. I'd finish my days sloppin' out for some young calico queen.'

'You could go back to Pittsburgh.'

'To what?' she snapped. 'Sellin' my body on the streets? I'd be dead at forty from some terrible disease.' She shook her head furiously. 'This ain't a bed of roses but I'm stayin'.' In her anger spittle had appeared at the corners of her mouth, and she dabbed at it with a square of muslin.

Harding looked at her for several seconds. 'Forgive me, Mrs Pierce. I guess I wasn't thinkin' straight,' he said, his voice soft. 'You say that Pierce wants to talk with me. Do you know what he's gonna say?'

She shook her head. 'He just sent me to tell you. He had

the notion that if he came here you might try an' throw him in jail.'

Harding smiled grimly. 'Yeah, I coulda done that.' He glanced at the clock. 'I'll give him ten minutes to say his piece. I'll be along in a while.'

Beth Pierce bit her lip. 'Will you walk across with me now? He'll be mad at me if you don't.'

'An' I'm guessin' he'll make you pay.'

She looked away from Harding, her teeth worrying the corner of the muslin, and nodded, her face flushing.

Harding stood up, pushing his journal into the top drawer of his desk. He reckoned it would be a waste of his time listening to Pierce, but Beth Pierce, ironically, brought back happy memories of his first days appearing for the defence in front of a judge. If walking into the saloon helped her even in a small way he would. Anyways, Pierce wouldn't be stupid enough to have him shot down there.

A few minutes later he followed Beth through the batwing doors of the Silver Lode. 'The stairs at the end,' she said. 'You take the hall an' it's the second door on the right. You'll see Big Harry. He's not very bright but he's one of the few decent men in this place. He'll take that gun-belt off you before you see Jake.'

'He's a careful man, your Mr Pierce.'

'I'll see you again, Mr Harding. Come and play cards sometime.'

'I'll do that,' Harding said, having no intention of doing so. He was damned if he was going to lose his money to some passing cowboy. He crossed the saloon to the stairs and went up to the open corridor which gave a view over the whole saloon.

One of the biggest men Harding had seen for a while sat on a chair outside the second door on the right of the corridor. Across his knees was a scatter-gun. He stood up as

Harding approached and leaned the scatter-gun against the wall.

'Howdy, Mr Harding. I hear you're a friend o' Miss Beth.'

'That's right. We knew each other in Pittsburgh.'

'A fine lady, Miss Beth. I reckon it's a real shame.'

Harding frowned. 'Why d'you say that?'

The big man looked around furtively. 'I guess I shouldna be talkin' like this, but I guess Miss Beth ain't gonna be with us too long. Now that Mr Pierce's gonna be a politician he's lookin' 'round for a mite younger gal.' A worried expression suddenly showed on his face. 'You ain't gonna tell Mr Pierce I said that?'

'I'll not say a word, Harry.' Harding's hand dropped to the buckle of his gun-belt. 'Miss Beth told me you'd take this.'

'Lose my job if I didn't,' Big Harry said, reaching out a hand as big as an old dog-house stirrup.

'Then you'd best take this as well,' Harding said, reaching behind his neck to pull from its sheath his throwing knife.

'Holy cow! I coulda missed that. I'm obliged to you, Mr Harding.'

Harding nodded pleasantly in return. He'd brought Big Harry on to his side, he reckoned, even if the good-natured man had missed the .22 pocket pistol tucked beneath his vest and the knife in his boot.

Harry placed Harding's gun-belt on the chair, knocked twice on the door behind him and opened it to allow Harding to enter the room. Pierce didn't move from behind his desk. He wore an expensive Prince Albert coat over a silk vest. In the light from the window his diamond ring twinkled in the sunlight and between the strong looking fingers of his other hand he held a fat cigar, the smoke curling and twisting up to the yellowy-white stucco ceiling.

'Come on in, Mr Harding. Take a seat.'

To the right of Pierce's desk in a wide wooden chair lounged a figure dressed from head to foot in black, his Stetson tilted so far forward that Harding had difficulty in seeing the man's face other than the lean jaw and rat-trap mouth. At his hip was a .45 Colt Army revolver with its 5½ inch barrel. The iron couldn't have been more than two years old, Harding realized.

'This gentleman here,' Pierce said, 'is Mr Mather. He rode into town a coupla days ago to help me with my business interests.'

Harding looked across to Mather but, save for a twitch of his chin, Mather appeared to ignore the introduction.

'He don't look like a bookkeeper,' Harding said. He looked back at Pierce. 'What is it you've got to say?'

Pierce took a long pull on his cigar. 'I gotta proposition for you, Sheriff.'

'I'm listenin'.'

'How much does a lawman make? Three hundred dollars a month, no more, I bet. In a town like Jackson Creek, I guess the mayor ain't payin' you more than a coupla hundred.' Pierce took the cigar from the corner of his mouth. 'You ride along with me, an' you'll be a rich man in a coupla years. I ain't tryin to bribe you, but I promise you'll see more money than you can even think of. By next spring you'll have enough to build a fine house for that little lady o' yourn.'

'Hold it there, Pierce, I've already heard enough. You're wastin' your time.' Harding got up from his chair, glaring down at Pierce. 'An' I don't like the way you speak of Miss Amy Dawson.' He heard Mather snicker from beneath his tilted Stetson, and turned to face him. 'I'm tellin' you now, Mather. You draw that Army Colt in this town, even if it's to knock in a nail, an' you'll die in Jackson.'

Slowly, Mather tipped back his Stetson. Harding saw that

a scar from an old knife fight ran from the corner of his eye to his ear. Mather's cold eyes hardened as he returned Harding's glare, unflinching. His mouth twisted.

'Mebbe I'll not need to now,' he said.

Harding walked back to the office angry with himself for reacting as he did when Amy was mentioned. In the West, even gunslingers kept women out of their business. But maybe Mather was an exception. If the gunman made even a move towards Amy, to hell with evidence and a judge, he'd shoot Mather down.

In the office he left Charlie to remind Seb Haines to search Frenchie's cage before giving him his dinner, and walked up to the livery while turning over his thoughts. Frenchie wasn't going to give trouble. He'd been told what would happen if he tried to make a run from Seb when he was taken out to the privy. But Charlie was maybe right when he recalled that Frenchie had been a miner, and Pierce needed him. That meant Pierce was guessing the Army gold had been hidden close by, possibly in the old coal tunnels. Could Pierce have killed the Englishman trying to make him talk?

He was still trying to get a handle on everything as he rode out to the Dawson house. It was a short ride, situated a few hundred yards past the last building of the town's Main Street, set in three or four acres of meadow.

Harding found an imposing building which showed that the man who built it had money when it was first erected. But Harding could see, as he secured his roan to the hitching rail, one or two places needed an extra lick of paint and the ground close to the house needed more attention than it seemed to be getting. Whoever was behind the wide entrance door must have seen him arrive. The door was opened as Harding reached the top of the steps.

'Welcome to the Dawson house, Mr Harding. My name is Felix.'

The speaker was a tall man, his features so black that his forehead was almost purple. He was immaculately dressed in a black tailed coat, over a white cotton shirt and grey crease-free pants.

'What brings you west, Felix?'

'The late Master Henry was a captain in the 54th Massachusetts Volunteers.'

'A regiment of loyal black soldiers, I recall.'

'That is correct, sir.'

'An' I'm guessin' you were his sergeant.'

Felix smiled and inclined his head. 'I had that honour, sir. Master Henry and I fought together until he fell at Fort Wagner.' He paused, a sad smile on his face. 'If you follow me, I shall show you to Miss Amy. She is in her study.'

Harding raised his eyebrows. Study? Amy was turning out to be full of surprises. Felix led him across a wide entrance hall and along a short passageway. Behind a door on the right came the sounds of a machine. Felix knocked on the door and, seemingly hearing an answer from within, opened the door.

'Sheriff Harding is here, ma'am.'

Harding heard her say, 'Show him in, Felix,' as the manservant stepped back from the door to allow Harding to enter.

'Good morning, Amy.' He shot a puzzled look at the metal box which sat on the table in front of her. 'What have you there?'

'A typewriter. I bought it in Boston.'

'An' what does it do?'

'Come and see.' She held up a sheet of paper. 'There's no need any more for a pen and ink; this machine can print words. The young ladies in Boston are beginning to use them in offices.'

'You mean young ladies are leaving their homes and working?'

'Yes, they think it much better than sitting in some parlour learning to play the piano badly or to speak a little French.' She shot him a sharp look. 'Don't tell Mother, but I worked in a newspaper office for two days.'

Amy, it appeared, was full of surprises but he thought it better to focus on the purpose of his visit, than to puzzle over her plans for the future. After all, maybe he'd have a say in what she was considering.

'You've something to show me?'

'Yes, I have.' She stood up and crossed the room to her cloth reticule. She took out a small metal object and held it up. 'I don't know what this is but it appears unusual for Robert Dale to have had it. I think it's something a soldier might wear, and I know Mr Dale had not been a soldier.'

'Let me see that.'

Harding took from her the metal object and placed it on the palm of his hand to examine it closely. The silver-coloured metal was tarnished but he had no difficulty in recognizing the shape of the eagle at what he assumed was the top of the object.

'I've seen one of these before,' he said slowly. 'You're right, it is an Army badge but exactly who would wear it I can't recall.' He looked up at Amy. 'Dale never mentioned this to you?'

She shook her head. 'He showed me many rocks but never this badge.'

'Old Zack might know something. Why don't we ride out or take your surrey and see him? Charlie told me he has a cabin off the trail to the homesteads. I need to take a look at the old tunnels and speak with the homesteaders. That's if your mother approves,' he added quickly.

Amy hesitated, and to Harding's surprise her face turned pink. But he quickly realized her concern was not about her mother when she spoke.

'Is there a reward for finding the gold?'

'I reckon so. A sizeable one I'd guess.'

'If we found the gold could I claim a share of the reward?'

'I'm not sure the gold's there to be found, but yes, you could.'

'And could you?'

He shook his head. 'No, but I'll explain later. I reckon we should be getting along.'

Baskins was only too pleased to be relieved of his duties when Harding explained that he'd drive Miss Dawson in the surrey that morning. Within half an hour Baskins had the surrey outside the front of the house, and despite Henrietta Dawson saying that she thought Amy was being a little fast riding out alone with Sheriff Harding, the two of them were soon sitting alongside each other as they headed for the homesteads.

'We'll call on Old Zack and ask him about the metal badge,' Harding said as he guided the pony at a good pace along the trail leading to the homesteads.

'You found nothing else out of the ordinary?'

'Nothing.'

Harding shrugged. 'There was just a chance we'd find an answer.' He raised his whip to point across a meadow. 'Is that Old Zack's place?'

'Yes, that's it.'

Pulling back the reins gently he turned the surrey to bounce across the bunch and buffalo grass. After twenty yards or so the surrey ran more smoothly over a dirt track which led to the cabin. Old Zack might lead a solitary life but he appeared to have made it as easy as possible. Harding brought the pony to a halt five or six yards from the door to the cabin. He tied the reins to the brake lever.

'Wait here,' he said. 'I'll be a few minutes.'

He knocked on the door, although he was beginning to doubt if Old Zack was inside. Surely he would have heard them approach and come out to greet them. Harding pushed at the door, which swung open.

'Zack! Sheriff Harding here.'

He waited a few seconds, and then stepped into the cabin. The interior was a pleasant surprise. Everything was scrupulously clean, as if someone like Lucy took care of the place. The late morning sun twinkled on a couple of brass pots. The rough-hewn table appeared to have been scrubbed that morning. There was a clean curtain at the end of the single-room cabin which Harding guessed hid Zack's bunk.

On a table, in a wooden frame, was a daguerreotype of a young soldier holding a long gun in a uniform different from the old Confederate butternut or the blue of the Union. Harding guessed it could have been an English uniform. There was nothing for him here, he decided. Old Zack, he'd heard, didn't stray far from his cabin, so he'd probably be back the following day.

Harding went outside. Over to his right an old grey stood in a small corral munching at the grass. Old Zack must have two horses, he realized. In Wyoming no man went afoot.

'He's not here,' he told Amy as he took back the reins. 'We'll go on to the homesteads.'

Back on the trail they were both silent, content with each other's company, as Harding allowed the pony to walk along at its own pace. His thoughts were on what Amy had found in the Englishman's boxes. Where had it come from? It was unlikely that Dale had brought it from England. There was something else that nagged him about the Englishman, something that he should have remembered. Maybe if he didn't think too hard, it would come to him. His thoughts were interrupted by a rider travelling fast, approaching them from a bend in the trail.

'Feller's ridin' hard,' he said.

The rider, reaching them, reined in his horse abruptly, the animal skittering across the ground. 'Sheriff!' The man barked. 'I was on my way into town to see you.'

As if suddenly remembering his manners, he pulled at the brim of his expensive hat. 'Miss Amy, I swear you look prettier every day.'

'Thank you, Mr Yorke. Sheriff, this gentleman is Mr Henry Yorke,' she added formally, 'Mr Yorke is owner of the Green Valley ranch.'

Yorke, aged around fifty, but still looking strong and healthy, cut into Harding's attempt to greet him politely. 'And I intend to remain so, whatever tricks that rogue Pierce gets up to.'

'What's the problem, Mr Yorke?'

'Pierce is buying out the homesteaders, an' takin' control of the land this side of the river. His wife's a fine woman but I got no time for him. He's after the whole stretch of the old open range, including the coal tunnels, an' that means he could cut off my cattle from water in high summer.'

'I'll take a look. Is Pierce there?'

'No, just that four-flusher lawyer, Miller, an' some feller in black. Looks like a gunslinger to me.' He half-turned the head of his mount. 'I'll ride back with you.'

'No need for that. Best if I talk with 'em without you. I'll let you know what I find out.'

The rancher hesitated for a moment, and then nodded. 'Mebbe you're right. But you tell Pierce that I got plenty of ex-soldiers among my cowboys. Gunplay ain't gonna scare 'em when I bring my beef to the river. An' I'll do that whatever

Pierce says.' He touched the brim of his hat. 'Good to see you again, Miss Amy.'

Harding flicked the reins to urge the pony on at a trot. The surrey made rapid progress and they soon passed the bend in the river where Harding had helped Amy and Baskin. The spring rain and the melted snows had raised the level of the water several inches and the waters were flowing fast.

A couple of miles on and Harding could see a cluster of men standing near the wooden posts of the most easterly homestead. When the surrey was a few hundred yards further on he recognized the figure of Mather standing alongside a heavily built man who looked out of place in a derby hat and city clothes. With them was gathered a crowd of a dozen or so men, most of whom wore blue bib coveralls and unusually wide-brimmed straw hats.

'I saw hats like those on the sailors in Boston,' Amy said.

'Stay where you are,' Harding told Amy. 'I know Mather. I'm guessing that's Pierce's lawyer.'

'Yes,' said Amy. 'My dear late father said he has the morals of a rattlesnake.'

'I'll remember that,' Harding said. He brought the surrey to a halt close to the men, secured the reins and stepped down to the ground. Before he had chance to greet the men Mather turned around to face him.

'Howdy, Sheriff,' he said, a malicious glint in his eyes. 'I see you've brought the little lady with you.'

Harding ignored him. It wasn't the time or the place to take on Mather. Instead, he turned to Miller. 'Howdy, Mr Miller. You mind tellin' me what's goin' on here?'

'It's all very simple, Mr Harding. These men are selling their homesteads to Mr Pierce.' His oily smile stayed in place for only a fraction of a second. 'You got any problem with that?'

Instead of replying directly Harding turned to the cluster of men standing nearby. 'Any man here who speaks for you all?'

A tall, broad-shouldered man whose muscles bulged beneath his shirt sleeves stepped forward. 'Name's Brenton, Sheriff.'

'Do I call you Cap'n or Bosun?'

The cluster of men burst out laughing, and one of them called out. 'Nailed you there, Harry!'

Brenton grinned. 'Cap'n's too fine for me, Sheriff. Bosun will be fine.'

'Bosun it is. How long you had these homesteads?'

'Coupla years, I guess.' He shrugged. 'Truth be told, we ain't doin' too well at this homesteadin'.'

'You all ex-sailors?'

'Every man jack.'

'I know where you're going with this, Sheriff.' Miller looked at him shrewdly. 'I'd heard you knew something of the law. More than a town's sheriff is likely to know.'

Again Harding addressed Brenton. 'Every man here served more than five years?'

Before Brenton could reply, Miller answered. 'Every man, Sheriff.' He thrust forward a sheaf of papers. 'Fourteen Military Land Warrants. You want to look them over?'

Harding shook his head. He knew he'd be wasting his time. He looked around and could see the half a dozen abandoned tunnels close to the river, all of them within the homestead areas. If the Army gold was hidden in one of them, Pierce would have time on his side to carry out a search.

'Seems OK to me, Mr Miller. When do the homesteads legally belong to Pierce?'

'Tomorrow noon.'

'Seems you came along too late,' Mather said, triumph

79

written across his face. 'You shouldn't have dallied with the pretty lady.'

Again Harding resisted the temptation to reply. He turned to Brenton. 'Bosun, I'd like a word.' He stepped away from the group of men, leading Brenton until they were out of earshot.

'I need to take a look at one of those tunnels,' he said. 'The one on your land would be fine. If I came out a coupla hours afore noon, the land is still yours an' everything would be legal.'

Brenton frowned, and then shrugged. 'Fine by me, Sheriff. You gonna tell me what you're after?'

They both looked up as Miller and Mather rode past. 'Sure is a fine lookin' lady,' called Mather.

Harding stared at the two men as they rode away. He'd need to settle with Mather. He turned back to Brenton. Bosun looked a good, honest man, and he didn't wish to lie when he answered Brenton's question. 'I can't tell you that yet. As soon as I learn somethin' for sure I'll tell you.'

Brenton looked at him for a few seconds before nodding. 'OK, I'll meet you by the tunnel a coupla hours after dawn. Mr Dale put new ladders in all the tunnels so we'll be OK, an' I'll bring a coupla lamps.'

'Did Dale ever say what he'd found?'

Brenton shrugged. 'A heap o' rocks is all I saw.'

'I'm obliged, Bosun. It would be better if you said nothing, not even to your wives.'

Brenton gave a short laugh. 'We're all on our own, Mr Harding. We were plannin' on sendin' for mail-order brides. Wrote to the *Matrimonial News* in San Francisco only two weeks back. Guess we're gonna have to think agin. We sure will never make farmers. Maybe we can set up a coupla stores or somethin' in town.'

The two men walked back to where Amy sat in the surrey

talking with a couple of the Navy men. As Harding approached, they touched the brims of their straw hats, nodded to Harding, and moved away.

'They saw Mather was bothering me, and came to the rescue,' she said.

With a hand raised in farewell, Harding stepped up to the surrey and took up the reins. He turned the pony and headed back to the trail for Jackson Creek.

'Why did you ask how long the men had served?' Amy asked.

'Homestead Act of 1862. Men who served at least five years in the Army or Navy aren't bound to spend five years improving the land they're given. They can sell when they choose.'

'Beth Pierce told me you were once a lawyer back East.'

Again, Amy had surprised Harding. 'You talk with her?'

'Why not? I see her in a store and we speak. She may be the wife of that brute Pierce, but that doesn't make her a bad woman.'

'I guess not.' The pony had slowed to a walk and he flicked the reins to urge her on. 'I was a lawyer for a time. Have you heard of the Molly Maguires?'

'Aren't they an Irish-American gang back East?'

'I sent six of them to prison, two of them to the hangman.' His mouth twitched. 'Their friends tried to kill me three times. I didn't want to try my luck again. Some of our fine citizens were going north, crossing the 49th and selling whiskey to the Indians. Ottawa formed the North West Mounted Police to hunt them down but they wanted an American with them. I volunteered.'

'But why are you now working in Wyoming?'

'Up north I was expecting to ride a desk in Ottawa.' He smiled, recalling his innocence. 'Instead for two years I rode a horse in the north-west. When the duty came to an end I

81

knew I'd never go back to a courtroom. Frank Warden was working in Cheyenne for John A. Campbell who was then the governor and they were looking for an extra man. I took the job but there was something I hadn't expected.'

'What was that?'

'I had to rejoin the Army.'

'But you're a sheriff!'

His mouth turned up. 'Yeah, it's a real barrel of tar.' He turned to smile at her. 'But here I am with you, and that makes everything worthwhile.'

She put out her hand to cover his. 'I'm glad,' she said.

'I'll ride out tomorrow and see Old Zack. Maybe he could—' he broke off suddenly.

'What's wrong?'

'I've remembered the badge you found. It's an eagle cockade. Soldiers who fought in the Mexican War of 1848 used to wear them in their caps.'

'But the ex-soldiers in town are much too young.'

'Yes, but Old Zack is old enough. I need to call on the *Clarion* again. Old Zack might not be who he claims to be.'

CHAPTER EIGHT

'Good morning, Mr Harding. Any more stories for us?' The shirt-sleeved genial figure of Hector Housman, at his desk behind a pile of newspapers, greeted Harding as the sheriff entered the office of the *Clarion*.

'Not today, Mr Housman. I need to check a name on the report the schoolmarm found for me.'

'The one on the gold robbery,' Housman said, pulling open a drawer in his desk. 'I gotta say, Sheriff, you get your teeth into somethin', you don't let go. Lucky I kept it.' He held up a strip of newsprint. 'What is it you want?'

'Just the name of the young soldier the Army never caught up with.'

'Hold on a moment.' Housman changed his spectacles and read from the strip. 'Isaac Holt. He was aged twenty, so he's probably still around.' He looked up, smiling, his gold tooth gleaming. ' 'Spect he's swannin' 'round Paris, France, if he made off with the gold.'

'Yeah, I guess so. I'm obliged, Mr Housman.'

Harding walked back to his office, returning the greetings of the townsfolk who still appeared to be pleased he was back in town. Some of the men gave him hard looks, and Harding guessed these were the men who were making money out of the store-owners driven out of Jackson by

Pierce's no-goods.

Could Old Zack be the young soldier who escaped? Until now he'd assumed 'Zack' was short for Zacharias, the same as for his boss down in Cheyenne. But supposing instead Zack was short for Isaac? It was in common use, the old man's age fitted and he'd been a soldier. Could he have fled north after the robbery and joined the English Army?

He'd seen plenty of their soldiers when he'd been with the Mounted Police – that's how he thought the uniform worn by the young man in the daguerreotype was vaguely familiar. He turned into his office.

'C'mon, Charlie,' he ordered his deputy. 'We'll give Bruno a run out to the homesteads.'

An hour or so later they reached Brenton's homestead. Both lawmen dismounted and led their horses across to where Bosun Brenton was standing a few yards from the opening of the tunnel. In his hand he held two lanterns.

'Howdy, Mr Brenton. This feller here is Charlie Wilson, my deputy.'

'Howdy.' He looked down at Bruno. 'Heck of a dog. Can he climb a ladder?'

Charlie grinned. 'He'll be fine here. He can watch the horses.'

Brenton gave one of the lanterns to Harding. 'I'll go down first. I've done it before, an' I can light the way. The ladder's safe enough but keep watch for any rocks we could start fallin'.'

'We'll secure our horses to that fence post, if that's OK with you.'

Brenton shrugged. 'Don't matter no more, I guess.' He placed his lantern on the ground to light it while Harding and Charlie secured the horses, fixing the reins so the animals could nibble at the grass. Bruno lay flat on the ground, eyeing the three men.

'You stay here, Bruno,' ordered Charlie.

'OK, here we go,' Brenton said, holding up the lamp, now lit, and stepping from the timbers that surrounded the entrance on to the top rung of the ladder. As Brenton began to climb down the ladder, Harding followed with Charlie stepping on to the ladder once Harding was clear.

The yellow light from the lamp cast shadows on the tunnel walls on either side of the men and Harding saw the remains of timbers that had once supported the sides of the tunnel. Successive winters had caused the timbers to begin crumbling.

Harding looked up past Charlie, and saw that the light from the open air above them was beginning to fade and he realized the rung he'd taken a few moments before had altered the line of their descent.

'All OK up top?' Brenton called out.

'We're fine, Mr Brenton. How much further?'

'Ten or fifteen yards maybe.' As Brenton called up to the lawmen, there came the rustle of small animals scurrying away beyond the lights.

'Rats,' called up Brenton. 'Don't concern yourselves. The Englishman said they always make a run for it.'

'I ain't sure this suits my pistol,' called Charlie. 'But I guess it beats workin' in a store.'

Harding's laugh echoed around the space. 'Keep thinkin' like that, Charlie.'

'OK, I'm at the bottom,' called Brenton.

Another half a dozen rungs and Harding stepped off the ladder and on to solid ground. He waited for a few moments until Charlie reached the last rung and stepped off the ladder with a sigh of relief.

'Guess I'd never make a miner,' he said sheepishly.

Harding turned to look around, Brenton holding his lantern high. The yellow light shone on the walls of the chamber around them, the layers of soil and rock clearly marked out. From inside a cave-like opening no more than five feet high and five or six feet wide came the rustle of small animals.

'The miners began to dig that tunnel when they thought of bringing out coal.' Brenton shrugged. 'It just never happened, tho' why they didn't go on, I don't know.'

'How far does the tunnel go?'

'The Englishman told me it's about thirty yards which takes it close to the river. He and that old man went through there a coupla times. He told me that at the end it's a cave like this one.'

'I'm goin' in there,' Harding said.

'Fer cris'sakes, anythin' could be in there,' exploded Charlie. 'Mebbe a mountain lion.'

'Then he'd haveta be able to climb the ladder,' Harding said. 'You two wait here. I'll be as fast as I can.'

'Give me that lantern, Sheriff, and we'll light them both,' Brenton said. He took a match from his bib pocket and a few moments later both lanterns were throwing their light around the rocky chamber.

Harding turned and, carrying one of the lanterns, ducked down to enter the cave. He kept his head low, trying to ignore the sounds of the rats scurrying out of the way of this trespasser entering their home. The strain on his knees was causing Harding to grimace as he followed the curving route of the tunnel. He winced as a small rock fell from above striking his shoulder.

Just as he was beginning to think the strain on his legs would prompt him to sit down and catch his breath he saw the roof of the tunnel slope upwards and as he went further forward he was gradually able to stand up straight. Five yards more and he stepped out of the tunnel and into a cave with its roof several feet above his head. He was much deeper underground than he'd first realized.

But he wasn't going further. Ahead of him was a wall of rocks, huge shapes resting on each other, as if thrown together by a giant's hand. He held up his lantern, searching to see if there was a way through but save for a small space, too small for a man to get through, the rock face was solid. If all the tunnels were like this, there was no chance that he would find any gold.

Harding raised his hand in farewell. 'Much obliged for your help, Bosun. We'll see you in town.'

The two lawmen turned the heads of their mounts, Bruno loping behind, keeping a wary eye on Harding's roan. A couple of days before he'd missed by inches a bad kicking when he'd snapped at the roan's rear hoofs.

'If the gold's in one of the old tunnels,' Harding said. 'I can see why Pierce needs a miner. There's no way those renegades woulda just buried it. They'd have blasted rocks on to it, plannin' to come back later.'

'Sheriff, I've bin thinkin',' Charlie said slowly, not looking directly across to Harding. 'You don't think we're wastin' our time with this gold? We ain't sure it's hereabouts, an' while we're searchin' Pierce could be up to anythin'.'

'You're thinkin' straight, Charlie. But why would Pierce buy the homesteads? He ain't plannin' to go sod-bustin' that's for sure. An' why send out Mather unless it was to make sure the homesteaders didn't back out? An' Miss Dawson found that eagle cockade I tol' you about. Sure, it could belong to Old Zack, but he's an old soldier, an' I reckon he'd hold on to it had he been in Mexico.'

'So where d'you think it came from?'

'I admit this is a wild guess, so don't you hold me to it. I reckon the Englishman found the gold and maybe old uniforms an' stuff. He took that—' Harding stopped suddenly, his horse veering closer to Charlie's mount. 'Charlie, s'posin' Dale took that cockade to show Wake as proof that he'd found the gold. An Englishman, a stranger in these parts, he wouldn't have a notion what to do. So he went to Wake to ask for advice. Wake wanted to see what Dale had found. That's why they were out ridin' together.'

Both horses had slowed to a walk while the men were speaking, and Harding gave his roan a nudge to pick up the pace. Behind them, Bruno was running backwards and forwards enjoying the smells he was finding amongst the grass and sagebrush.

'So why was Lawyer Wake attacked?' Charlie queried. 'Was it just happenstance an' some no-good got scared off afore he could steal a watch and purse?'

Harding shook his head. 'I said once afore, I don't believe in happenstance. But I'm gonna have to study on that some more. Right now, I can't give you an answer.'

'OK,' Charlie said. He pointed across a broad meadow. 'Old Zack's cabin.'

They broke from the trail to have their mounts lope towards the cabin and after a few hundred yards they reached the dirt track that Old Zack had made for himself. After ten yards, Charlie let out a shout, reined in his horse and pointed to the ground.

'There's blood here, lots of it. Somebody's been hurt real bad.'

The two men, their horses now at a walk, slowly made their way to Old Zack's cabin. Every few yards, Charlie would point down at the splashes of crimson that marked the dirt of the track. Finally they reached the cabin.

Harding pushed open the cabin door. 'You here, Zack?' he called.

There was no sound. Nothing moved. Then Harding looked at the scrubbed floorboards. Splashes of blood led from the doorway to the curtain which Harding assumed hid the old soldier's bunk. He heard the whisper of iron on leather behind him as Charlie drew his Colt. Avoiding the blood, Harding trod quietly across the cabin and pulled back the curtain.

'Jesus Christ!'

'That's Old Zack!' Charlie exclaimed behind him.

On the bunk lay the old man. His face was black with bruises, the flesh around his eyes puffed out so much that Harding could barely see his eyelids. But it was the old man's hand that lay like a mortally wounded animal on the rough blanket that had caused Harding to take a short step back. Alongside the wrinkled skin of the thumb four bloody stumps showed where the fingers had been hacked off.

'Fer cris'sakes,' swore Charlie. 'Is he alive?'

'I'm not sure.' A faint noise came from the old man and Harding bent down as he had on his second day in Jackson to listen to the few words of a dying man.

'Tell me, Zack,' he said urgently. 'Tell me who did this, an' I'll see him hang.'

The old man's voice was just strong enough for Harding to hear. 'The Angel of Death,' the old man muttered hoarsely. 'Dressed all in black. Death arrived.'

Harding took a deep breath. 'Mather,' he murmured to Charlie. He bent down to the bed again. 'And the gold, Zack? Did you find it?'

'Me an' the Englishm. . . .'

His voice trailed away, and his head slumped sideways. Harding couldn't see if Old Zack's eyes were closed but he brushed his hand over the swollen flesh. He stood up and turned to Charlie.

'We'll send someone from town,' he said. 'Then we'll go after Mather.'

CHAPTER NINE

'I've given a couple of the Navy men a dollar each to bring Old Zack back into town,' Charlie said, as he came through the doorway from the street. 'Mather's in the Lode. Sonovabitch goes for the whiskey after a killin'.' He sat down opposite Harding. 'Mather's gonna swing for this,' he said flatly, 'doin' that to an old man. Why the hell would he do it?'

'To make him talk,' Harding said. 'Pierce must have found out that Old Zack was Isaac Holt, the young soldier who escaped. Pierce musta believed Old Zack knew where the gold was hidden.' He breathed in deeply. 'An' back in Pittsburgh I saw another man with his fingers cut off to try an' make him talk.'

'An' I'm guessin' Pierce was involved.'

'Beth Pierce was charged with the man's murder.' Harding's mouth was set in a hard line. 'There could be honest folk in the Lode, an' we don't want 'em hurt. Here's what we do. We go in with our guns on our hips, an' try an' talk Mather out.'

'You think that's gonna work with a rattlesnake like Mather?'

Harding breathed in deeply. 'I guess not. But we're lawmen not butchers. A judge will hear what we have to say when the time comes.'

'OK, I got that.'

'We go into the Lode and split up. You go left, I go right. If Mather goes for his gun we shoot to kill him. Don't give him a chance to come back on us.'

Charlie's face was stiff. 'You reckon he's real fast?'

'I don't know, but I guess so.' Harding looked across at Charlie. 'It's tougher facin' a gunfight cold. Not like when you're boilin' mad.'

'You're damned right, Mr Harding.' Charlie's hands dropped to his gun-belt to settle it snugly on his hips. 'OK, I'm ready.'

Harding got up from his desk. Like Charlie he adjusted his gun-belt and then pulled on his hat. Together, the two lawmen went out to the street and crossed the hardpack, heading for the Silver Lode. A young woman carrying a basket smiled a greeting at the two men and appeared surprised as they merely nodded grimly in return.

Harding pushed through the batwing doors of the saloon and immediately moved to his right. Charlie entered close behind. Both men stood motionless looking to the centre of the saloon where Mather sat playing cards with the Mexican barman. They were the only two in the saloon.

'Pablo!' Harding called out. 'Get behind the bar! Charlie,' he called, 'Pablo reaches for that scatter-gun he keeps under the bar afore we leave, shoot him.'

'No, no, *señor*!' The barkeep jumped from his chair and scuttled away from the table to stand behind the bar looking fearfully across at Charlie, his hands plainly in sight in front of him.

Mather looked across at Harding. 'You're spoilin' my game, Sheriff. Pablo an' me like our three-card monte when honest folks are about their work.' He spread the three cards on the table, his hands moving so rapidly it was difficult to detect which card fell where.

Mather's mouth curved in a cruel smile. 'You wanna come an' choose the ace, Sheriff?' He paused for a second and then turned up a card to show the ace of spades. 'You gotta know, Sheriff, now you've seen it. I'm really fast with my hands. Faster than you, I reckon, an' that goes for the kid deputy o' yourn.'

'Mather, I'm putting you in jail to wait for the judge.'

'Oh, yeah? An' what you gonna be doin' that for?'

'Fer killin' Old Zack. You made a mistake, Mather. He lived long enough to tell us. A dyin' man's words go a long way afore a judge an' jury.'

Mather's expression didn't change. He stood up slowly, his hand dropping to the butt of his sidearm. 'I hate killin' lawmen, makes all your partners with a badge real ornery.'

They were the last words he'd ever speak. The heavy slug from Harding's Colt shattered the front of his skull, blood and grey matter spraying over the cards on the table. His lifeless torso was hurled back, sending the chair spinning, his body slamming against the sawdust covered floor.

'*Madre de Dios!*' Pablo was crossing himself furiously, his brown face almost pale with shock.

'Pablo, tell Pierce it's his mess to clean up,' Harding called out. He looked across to his deputy. Charlie stood motionless, his face taut, his Colt held loosely down by his leg. 'Let's get outa here, Charlie.'

Five minutes later Harding was back behind his desk and Charlie was pouring coffee from the pot on the stove, his face pale and his hand trembling slightly. Harding opened the bottom drawer of his desk and pulled out a bottle. As Charlie brought over the coffee Harding uncorked the whiskey and took a long pull. He wiped the neck of the bottle with his sleeve and handed the bottle over.

'Take a slug o' that, Charlie. Killin' a man ain't easy, even a no-good like Mather. It's different in war, an' when you're with partners agin other men, but cold killin' ain't ever gonna be somethin' you'll get used to. An' if it does then you're a lost soul.'

Charlie picked up the bottle and took a gulp. 'Pierce woulda killed me that first day you came into town. I know that now.'

'Yeah, I reckon.'

Harding looked up as the door opened and Amy Dawson entered the office. Harding jumped to his feet, and Charlie hid the bottle behind his back, moving across the office to place it in a corner where it couldn't easily be seen by their unexpected visitor.

Harding went around the desk and pushed a chair forward for Amy to sit down. 'We've seen one of the tunnels,' he explained, after greetings had been exchanged between the three. 'If the Army gold is in one of them, Pierce has time on his side.'

For a second his mind dwelled on his likely reception when he eventually returned of his own free will to Cheyenne. Even worse, when Governor Thayer maybe sent men to find out why he'd disobeyed a lawful order. 'But what brings you into town so early?'

Amy opened her reticule and pulled out a book kept closed by two short strings halfway down its length. 'An hour ago I found this on the top of a shelf. There's no marking of his name so it hadn't been packed into Mr Dale's boxes but I recognized it as the one he wrote in daily.'

Harding felt his muscles tighten. He realized now that the journal, or rather its absence, had been the question nagging him at the back of his mind. He should have remembered more clearly as Amy had mentioned the journal when he first went to her house. 'Does it have anything about finding the gold?'

Amy shook her head. 'I don't know. I haven't had time to open it.' She handed it across the desk. 'I decided to bring it straight to you.'

Harding took the journal from her and undid the strings. If Dale had followed his normal practice and recorded everything he did during his day, then the journal should contain the precise location of the stolen gold. Watched by Amy and Charlie he opened the journal.

'Goddamnit!' He looked up quickly at Amy. 'Forgive my bad language,' he said.

Her face a little pink, Amy looked puzzled. 'What's wrong?'

Harding held up the journal so that the other two could see the open journal. Every page was blank. Not one word had been written in the journal by Robert Dale.

'If the Englishman did find the gold he didn't record it.' He frowned. 'Amy, you're sure Dale wrote only in a journal like this?'

She nodded. 'I'm sure. I recognized the journal as soon as I saw it.'

A grim smile appeared on Harding's face. 'I'll wager Dale carried a coupla these journals, maybe more.' He turned to his deputy. 'Charlie, escort Miss Dawson to where she wishes to go. I'll be back soon, but first I have to see Doc Radman.'

Radman shook his head in response to Harding's question. 'Josh is not goin' to make it. The blackguard who attacked him has committed murder. I doubt if Josh will last a coupla days.'

Harding hesitated. He'd been warned when he'd told Amy and Charlie what he was about to do, that Radman could be difficult about his patients. He permitted nothing that would cause them distress. If Wake was so close to his last moments Radman might well refuse Harding's request to ask him further questions.

'Doc, I know this is hard. But I need to ask Mr Wake just one question. I'll not ask more.'

Radman looked out of the window for a few seconds, apparently considering his decision before he looked back at Harding. 'I have your word, Sheriff, that this is important?'

'You have my word.'

Radman stood up. 'OK, one question. Follow me.'

Harding followed the doctor into the sickroom. Wake lay on his back, his face ashen, save for the dark shadows beneath his eyes. Harding could see that since his previous visit the flesh of the lawyer's face was shrinking back to the bones of his head. Harding didn't need be a doctor to recognize that the man on the bed would probably soon be dead. With a flourish of his hand, Radman indicated that Harding should go ahead. His head bent close to the lawyer's mouth, Harding asked his question.

'Mr Wake, what became of the Englishman's journal?'

There was no answer from Wake and Harding opened his mouth to ask the question again. Then he caught the faint whisper of Wake's voice.

'He stole the journal.'

For an instant he was tempted to ask more questions but then the hand of the doctor fell on his shoulder. 'That's all, Sheriff. Now let Josh die in peace.'

'I'm obliged to you, Doc,' Harding said when the two men had quit the sickroom. He left the doctor's rooms, thinking hard as he walked along the boardwalk back to his office.

He didn't have to break into a sweat to work out that Dale must have put the record of his findings into the lawyer's hands when they'd ridden out together. The Englishman had another journal back at the Dawson house which he'd intended to start the following day. But by then he was dead and the journal Amy had found had never been written in.

Regardless of who had attacked the lawyer the order would have come from Pierce who must now have the Englishman's journal. But Charlie was probably right. The gold would have been well hidden and Pierce would need a miner to uncover it. That was the reason for trying to free Frenchie. He reached his office, and entering, was surprised to see Amy still present.

'I've been talking with Mr Wilson about his sister,' she explained. 'Maybe one day she could join Felix – I'd be happy to train her. Were you successful?'

'As we suspected, Dale gave the lawyer his journal for safe-keeping but it was stolen when Wake was attacked.'

'So Pierce now has the Englishman's journal,' Charlie said flatly.

'I guess so. But I've an idea how we can get hold it. Amy, I need your help.'

She answered immediately. 'What do you wish me to do?'

'I need to talk with Beth Pierce. You said once that you speak when you meet in a store. Could you get her to come to my clapboard?'

'I'll try.'

'Could you manage to see her today?'

'I think so. She often goes to the dry goods store around noon.'

'Fine. When she comes to the clapboard I'd feel easier if you were there, too. And bring her in at the back door. I don't want one of Pierce's no-goods seeing her.'

'I'll be there.'

'Charlie, warn Matt Parkes we'll need his fastest horse back o' my clapboard by noon today or maybe we'll have to wait for tomorrow. I'll see him later.'

'I'll fix that, Mr Harding.'

Harding glanced across at the old railroad clock. If he rode his roan hard he could reach the Green Valley ranch and be back in Jackson by noon.

'OK, let's get movin'.'

Harding stood up from his chair when he heard the knocking at the rear of his clapboard. Half a dozen strides took him to the door, and he moved aside as first Beth Pierce, and then Amy, stepped through the doorway.

'Anyone see you?'

Amy shook her head. 'Beth tells me all Pierce's men are eating now.'

'Fine. You two ladies take a seat.'

He waited until they had both settled, and then turned to Pierce's wife.

'Beth, I'm gonna need your help.'

She gave a wry smile. 'You haven't called me "Beth", since Pittsburgh. What do you want me to do?'

Harding held up the journal Amy had found. 'Pierce has a journal like this.'

Beth nodded. 'I've seen it.'

'Do you know where it's kept?'

'Yes.'

'I want you to take it and bring it to me.'

Beth leaned back, her eyes wide. For a few moments there was total silence. Then she spoke. 'I can't do that. He'd know it was me. He'd throw me to that pack of animals who work for him. I'd be lucky to stay alive.'

'I've thought of that. You bring the journal to me, and I'll make sure you're safe.'

Beth's face flushed red with anger. 'You're not thinkin' straight, Mr Harding! You think putting me in some clapboard with a guard on the door will stop my husband? Or are you suggestin' again I leave Jackson? I tol' you what would happen to me.' Tears began to run down her cheeks, and she fumbled at her skirt for muslin to dab at her eyes. 'The day I walked outa that courtroom away from you I swore I'd never break the law again. An' I never have. I'm not stealin', even for you.'

'It's not stealing, Mrs Pierce,' Amy said quietly. 'That journal belonged to Robert Dale, and his family in England should have it. Mr Dale believed his findings would be important to science, and there are men in England who will understand what he has written.'

Beth swung around in her chair. 'Oh, Miss Dawson, don't you understand? I take that journal and I'll be made to pay.'

'Not if I take you away from Jackson,' Harding said. 'Henry Yorke at the Green Valley ranch will give you shelter.'

'Henry Yorke? Why would he do such a thing? He hardly knows me. He's been in the Lode with his cowboys, but he doesn't stay long. He drinks a coupla whiskies, plays a few hands, and then he leaves. Why would he. . . ?' Her voice trailed away, a puzzled look on her face.

'He thinks you're a fine woman, Beth. He told me himself this morning when I rode out to the ranch. You'll be safe with him.'

'He'll not send me back?'

Harding smiled. 'He's hopin' you'll stay.'

Beth looked at them both for several moments. Then she nodded.

'I'll do it,' she said. 'I'll get you the journal, but I don't know when.'

'Can you ride 'cross a horse?' Harding asked.

Beth's mouth twitched. 'Smart ladies like Miss Dawson ride side-saddle. Sure, I can ride 'cross a horse.'

Harding stood up. 'You take care. Where's Pierce now?'

'Don't worry about him. He spends his afternoons with

one of—' She broke off and shrugged. 'I haven't cared for a while, I guess.'

Harding was writing in his journal when Charlie came back from his midday meal. 'Chinaman sure does great steaks, any bigger an' he'd haveta put a corral 'round 'em,' Charlie said, patting his stomach. 'He serves a great huckleberry pie, an' Bruno gotta bone.'

Harding looked across at the dog which had taken up its usual position a foot or so from the pot-bellied stove. 'Yeah, I reckon Bruno's still smilin'.'

Charlie frowned. 'Dogs don't smile, Mr Harding. They don't have—' He broke off suddenly, and waved a dismissive hand in the air. 'Aw, jumpin' rattlesnakes! You got me agin!'

Harding grinned, but was then serious. 'All quiet in town when you took a turn?'

'Four tough-lookin' *hombres* rode in from the east. I kept watchin' to see if they went straight to the Lode but they checked in at Bannon's place. Then they came across to the Chinaman's when I was eatin' my steak.'

'They could be goin' on to Cheyenne.'

'Yeah, I guess so.' Charlie frowned. 'There was somethin' about them which made me ponder on what they were doin' here.'

Both men turned to see Seb, a couple of plates in one hand, a tin mug in the other, limp through the doorway from the cages, his peg leg sounding on the boards.

'Frenchie OK?' Harding asked.

'Sure is, Sheriff. How long's he gonna be with us?'

'Too long. Judge ain't due for mebbe a month or so.'

'Keeps me workin' I guess. Gonna cost the town tho'.' Seb held up the plates. 'I'll take these back to the Chinaman.'

'Let's hope what you tol' me works out an' we get the journal,' Charlie said after Seb had left. 'I'll take a walk 'round town, make sure it's quiet.' He raised a finger to the brim of his hat in salute and went out into the street.

Harding poured himself coffee, thinking about Beth Pierce's chances of getting her hands on the Englishman's journal if not today, then as soon as she was able. He looked up from the pot as the street door opened and Mayor Bannon entered, closely followed by four men. All four were smartly dressed and looked prosperous. Their Colts, in holsters of shiny tooled leather, bore matching ivory-covered butts. Their Western suits and hats were stylish.

'Sheriff, these men are on the way to Cheyenne,' Bannon said. 'I told them about the prisoner you have here waitin' for the judge.'

The tallest of the four who appeared to be in charge pulled back his short trail coat to show the US marshal's badge on his vest. 'The name's Caxton, Sheriff. We spoke with Mr Bannon and explained we were ridin' through to Cheyenne, an' that's when he told us about the man you're holdin'.'

Harding frowned. 'So what's your interest in Frenchie?'

'We thought we'd do you a favour. Take Frenchie to Cheyenne an' the judge'll handle it there. Mr Bannon says it'll be cheaper for the town to have Mrs Fielding go to Cheyenne instead of the town payin' for this no-good Frenchie.'

'Sounds OK to me,' Harding said. 'How come we've never come across each other?'

'We've been down in Colorado,' said one of the men.

'My deputy said you came in from the east.' Harding shrugged. 'Guess he must have been mistaken.'

'No, your deputy had it right,' Caxton said. 'We had a job to do in Deadwood afore we headed for Cheyenne.'

Harding nodded. 'OK, pick up Frenchie an hour after dawn. An' I'll give you a letter for my boss, Zack Hogg.' He looked at Caxton. 'I s'pose you know Zack?'

'Sure do,' Caxton said easily. 'But if he hears you callin' him Zack he ain't gonna be too friendly.'

Harding grinned. 'No, I was fergettin'. He'd be as mad as a rattler.' He reached in his vest pocket, and pulled out a few coins. 'Do me a favour when you see him. Buy him a coupla whiskies from me.'

'Yeah, I'll do that.' Caxton picked up the cash. 'We'll be here after sunup. Have the prisoner ready to ride.'

'I sure will, Marshal. You're taking a load off the town.'

After the men had left, Harding sat behind his desk turning over his thoughts. After five minutes he stood up abruptly and, freeing his roan from the hitching post in front of the office, he stepped up to the saddle and rode to the outskirts of the town where he knew he'd find the homesteaders who had sold out to Pierce.

Bosun Brenton must have seen him arrive. The door to the old clapboard opened as Harding swung down from the saddle and Brenton walked down the short path to meet him.

'Howdy, Bosun. You all findin' town life to your likin'?'

Brenton jerked a gnarled thumb to point behind him. 'Place is fallin' down, an' the bunkin' space was bigger onboard the *WestDale*. But we'll fix things. The men are at the store, seein' what we need. What brings you here?'

'I need you all for a job. Say ten dollars each?'

'I'll get you the men,' said Brenton promptly. 'What is it you want doin'?'

Brenton listened carefully as Harding explained what he needed. The old sailor asked a couple of questions and once both men were satisfied that everything was clear, they shook hands. Harding rode back into town feeling much easier.

CHAPTER TEN

'Here they come,' said Charlie.

He turned away from the window and crossed to the chair by the stove at the rear of the office. He patted the head of Bruno who sat, unmoving, alongside him. Harding picked up his pen. On his desk was the paper releasing Frenchie to Caxton's custody. It could be the first thing Caxton asked for when he entered the office. The door from the street opened. Caxton and the three others filed in, Caxton halting in front of Harding's desk.

'Good day to both of you,' Caxton said cheerily. He looked across at Bruno. 'Hey, that really is some dog. Is he safe?'

'You don't have to worry about Bruno,' Charlie said.

Caxton turned to Harding. 'You all signed up for Frenchie to be taken away?'

Harding didn't move for a second, and then he looked up at Caxton.

'Moving your hands very slowly,' he said, 'take off that badge and put in on the desk. Any man reaches for a sidearm my deputy will shoot him in the back. He'll hate doin' it, but he has his orders.'

Caxton's jaw dropped. 'What the hell you sayin', Sheriff? I'm taken' your prisoner to Cheyenne, that's all.'

'I ain't gonna tell you agin, an' move real slow.'

A metallic sound broke the silence as Charlie cocked his sidearm.

'OK! I'm doin' what you say,' Caxton said quickly. 'But I still want to know what the hell you think you're about.' His hand moved to his vest and he unhooked the badge and placed it on the desk in front of Harding.

'You turnin' yellow, Caxton?' rasped the man nearest the window.

'Shut your mouth, Grimes,' barked Caxton, his eyes never leaving Harding.

'Now you all take off your gun-belts,' Harding said.

'We can take these small-town hayseeds,' rasped Grimes.

'You gonna choose to die for a few dollars from Pierce?' Harding said evenly. 'Or do you no-goods owe him a favour? Take a look in the street. Seven men with long guns at the front, seven at the back.'

'I can see 'em,' Grimes snarled. 'Every man a sod-buster.'

'Yeah, an' every man from the gun-deck crew of the USS *WestDale*. You ever hear what they did at Galveston? They ain't known for takin' prisoners.'

'I ain't dying here for Jake Pierce,' rasped Caxton. 'Take off your gun-belts,' he ordered the other three. 'You as well, Grimes,' he barked, as the man began to mutter. The four men slowly unbuckled their gun-belts, lowering them to the floor.

'OK, kick 'em behind you.'

All four did as they were told. Harding opened the drawer of his desk and took out his Navy Colt and set it on the desk before him. 'Now take off your boots.'

'What the hell d'you think you're about?' Caxton snarled.

'You got just three seconds before my deputy sets the dog on one of you. He ain't gonna be too fussy who he chooses.'

'Jesus Christ, Caxton!' the youngest of the four said. 'I

seen what a dog that big can do! OK, Sheriff, I'm takin' off my boots!'

Harding sat watching the four men, his hand loosely around the butt of his Navy Colt. 'OK,' Harding said, tightening his grip on his Colt and raising the barrel to point in Caxton's direction. 'Now take off your pants.'

'Go to hell!' Grimes shouted. 'I ain't takin' off my pants for—' His protest was cut off as Charlie's Colt smashed against the side of his neck, forcing him on to his knees.

'Get your pants off, you no-good sonovabitch or Bruno will tear your head off!'

Each man, hopping in front of the desk, took off his pants, shoving them back to Charlie who stuffed them into the sack on top of the gun-belts.

'You can put your boots back on,' Harding said. 'You're too much trouble for Jackson. The Navy men are gonna ride with you for half a day. Then you'll get your pants and guns back. That's your deadline. You ever cross it towards Jackson an' we'll shoot you on sight. No judge, no law, just a bullet. You take my advice an' quit the Territory. In a week lawmen from Cheyenne will be huntin' for a fake marshal.' He glared at each one in turn. 'Now get the hell outa my sight.'

The four men wordlessly turned to the door followed by Charlie, his Colt held down by his side as he watched while they mounted, their faces black with fury as the wave of laughter from the boardwalks swept over them. Some of the townsmen called out ribald remarks and the few women who were around so early stepped smartly into nearby stores trying not to exchange smiles.

Harding went through to the rear of the building and waved from the high barred window of the unoccupied cage to indicate that the seven Navy men at the rear should join their companions. He stepped down from the small stool, and heard Frenchie call across from the opposite cage.

'Sheriff, I gotta talk with you.'

Harding crossed the narrow passageway and saw that his prisoner was standing at the bars of the cage, a grim look on his face. 'What's up, Frenchie?'

'I know it ain't gonna change what happens down in Cheyenne, but I gotta see Mrs Fielding.'

Harding frowned. 'Mrs Fielding ain't gonna want to see you. What d'you want to see her for?'

Frenchie's teeth worried his bottom lip. 'I been thinkin' a lot in here. Like I said, I know it ain't gonna change anythin' but I'd like to say how sorry I am I offended her.'

Harding looked at his prisoner. Frenchie could just mean what he was saying, he decided. Anyways, what was there to lose? He doubted if Fielding's wife would agree to see Frenchie. But there was no harm in asking her.

'I'll ask her,' Harding said. 'That's all I can do.'

'I'm obliged to you, Sheriff.'

Harding went back into the office as his deputy came in from the street.

'Everything OK?'

'Yeah, those Navy men sure are tough when they've a job to do.' Charlie took off his hat and wiped the sweat off his face. 'Heck, that was mighty close a while back. I thought Bruno was gonna lick Caxton's hand. Coulda ruined everythin'.' He looked at Harding and frowned. 'You still ain't tol' me how you knew Caxton was a no-good.'

'He tried to be too smart. He made out he was a pardner o' my boss in Cheyenne. He musta heard about him gettin' real ornery when he was called "Zack". I asked Caxton to buy him a coupla whiskies, an' he agreed.'

'Nothin' wrong with that.'

Harding grinned. 'Zacharias Hogg is head of the Cheyenne Temperance League.'

Charlie pulled of his hat and with it smacked his thigh in delight.

'Jumpin' rattlesnakes! Ain't you the one, Mr Harding!'

They burst out laughing and then both looked to the street door, hearing the knock. Harding raised his eyebrows in Charlie's direction, and then shrugged.

'Come in,' he called. The door opened, and Lucy stood in the doorway. 'You don't haveta knock, Lucy,' Harding said. 'Scared us both, a knock on the door. Ain't that right, Charlie?'

'Aw, Mr Harding, you're joshin' me agin. Anyways, I come to tell you Mrs Pierce is in the clapboard waitin' fer you.'

Harding jumped to his feet, snatching up his trail jacket. 'Charlie, that horse from Parkes back o' the clapboard?'

'An' your roan.'

'Lucy, stay here an' talk with Charlie fer ten minutes,' Harding ordered. 'Charlie, I'll be back in a coupla hours.'

He walked the few yards to his clapboard to find Beth Pierce, her face pale, seated beside the table in the centre of the room. In her lap sat the Englishman's journal. Her head jerked in Harding's direction.

'Shut the door,' she implored. 'If anyone sees me I'm done for.'

'You're safe now, Beth. Does Pierce know what you've done?'

'I don't think so. He and some of his men have ridden out to the old homesteads.'

'OK, we're gonna go out to Green Valley.' He looked around the room, and then pointed at the small canvas sack at her feet. 'Is that all you got?'

'I don't want anything from that place,' she said bitterly.

'Give me the journal.' He took it from her and shoved it into the deep pocket of his trail jacket. 'We'll ride back o' the stores until we're at the end of town, then we'll hightail

106

it out to the ranch.'

Ten minutes later they kicked their horses on as they left the hardpack of Main Street and reached the trail heading north to the ranch. Beth hadn't been exaggerating when she'd told him she could ride across the saddle. His roan was hard pressed to keep up with the mount loaned by Parkes, and in a short time they put Jackson behind them.

A couple of times Harding was aware that Beth looked behind her, seemingly fearful that they would be followed, but when he, too, turned his head to study the trail they had covered there was no sign of any riders attempting to catch up with them.

A few minutes short of the hour they rode beneath the high wooden sign which marked the territory of the Green Valley ranch. Over to the east a group of three cowboys turned their horses to look across at the pair whose horses had been reined in to a walk, enabling them to rest after their fast gallop.

A mile further, a beaten track led Harding and Beth to the Big House of the ranch. Unusually, it boasted two storeys and steps leading to a high door set between two wooden pillars. Henry Yorke must have been given some notice of their arrival. The high door opened as Harding and Beth reined in, the horses blowing hard, moisture gleaming on their necks.

'Howdy, Mrs Pierce, Sheriff.' Yorke said, as he came down the steps. 'Welcome to Green Valley.'

Beth slipped easily from her saddle. Dust from the trail showed on her face, but her colour had returned, and Harding couldn't help thinking that she was a fine looking woman.

'Thank you for giving me shelter, Mr Yorke. But my name is Beth Maynard. I don't wish to hear the name of Pierce ever again.'

'Then Miss Maynard, it is. Or may I call you Beth?'

'Of course.'

'Then you must call me Henry.' He looked up at Harding. 'Will you take coffee while we find you another mount? One of my men will bring the roan back into town in a coupla days.'

'Coffee sounds fine. Your man will need to bring back Beth's horse. It belongs to the livery.'

'He'll do that. Now both of you come along.' Yorke looked at Beth as he saw her hesitate. 'What's wrong, Beth?'

'I'll not be a burden, Henry. I can cook an' sew—'

'Goodness me! I've people to do those tasks. You're here as my guest, Beth, and you'll be treated as one.' He breathed in deeply. 'Just smell that coffee!'

Almost two hours later Harding secured his mount to the hitching post in front of the fence to Amy's house. The grey loaned to him by Yorke was a strong animal and he'd made good time from the ranch. On the trail back to town he'd felt as if the Englishman's journal was burning a hole in his trail jacket but he'd resisted the temptation to bring the grey to a walk so he could open the book. Harding walked up to the entrance of the house and pulled at the bell-cord. A few moments later the door opened and the smiling face of Felix greeted him.

'Good day, Mr Harding. Miss Amy has just returned from her Ladies' Society.' Harding followed Felix along the hall to where a door opened into a large parlour. 'Sheriff Harding to see you, Miss Amy,' Felix announced.

'Clay! Do you have it?'

Her obvious excitement prompted a smile to show on his face. He thrust his hand into the deep pocket of his trail jacket, and pulled out the journal.

'Here it is!' He announced triumphantly. 'Let's hope we'll find out where the gold was hidden all those years ago.'

Amy patted the cushion beside her. 'Do come and sit down, and show me.'

'Your mother might—'

'Oh, jiminy! Maybe you had better sit over there.'

She pointed at the overstuffed chair opposite her. Smiling, Harding took his seat, untied the string which held the journal's covers and flicked through to the last page.

'I'll be d—'

He stopped before he swore, not wishing to have Amy think he often used bad language. His mouth was turned down as he looked across at her. 'He's written in code,' he said. He flicked through the last few entries. 'The last two pages are all in this crazy code.'

'Let me see,' Amy said, her expression registering her disappointment.

He handed her the journal, his thoughts racing. He considered himself an educated man. He knew Latin and mathematics but codes were beyond him. He would have to send the book to Cheyenne. Maybe someone in the governor's office could break the code and discover where the gold was hidden. But that would mean his losing a good reason for disobeying a lawful order and Amy losing any chances of the reward. He'd have to think hard before he decided how to proceed. He looked across to Amy and was surprised to see her smiling as she studied the journal.

'What is it?'

'This isn't a code, Clay. These last two pages are in shorthand.'

'I'm not following you.'

'Shorthand's a written system invented by an Englishman, James Pitman. A writer can keep up with the spoken word. Many young ladies in Boston are experts.'

'Maybe someone in Cheyenne knows how to read it.'

'That's not necessary. I may take a while, but I believe I

can.' Her smile broadened. 'I started to learn it in Boston during the winter, and Mr Dale gave me some lessons.'

Harding wasn't sure what his response should be. Amy Dawson was proving to be a hatful of surprises. He was used to gentlewomen knowing how to play the pianoforte, maybe being clever with watercolours or speaking French or Italian. He hadn't met one before who could use a machine that wrote letters like Housman used at the *Clarion* and read strokes and scratches that turned into spoken words.

'I'll be back tomorrow,' he said. 'Don't let that book out of your sight.'

CHAPTER ELEVEN

Fielding was cutting cloth with a large pair of shears when Harding walked in the dry goods store. He put down the shears and gave Harding his full attention.

'Good day to you, Sheriff. Are you lookin' for more shirts?'

'Not today, Mr Fielding. With your permission I'd like to have words with Mrs Fielding.'

The storekeeper raised his eyebrows. 'What about?'

'Frenchie, the man who attacked your wife wants to say how sorry he is.'

'The sonovabitch should be sorry. I hope he gets five years breaking rocks. One of Pierce's men came an' tried to buy me off. I told him to go to hell.'

'You were right to do so, Mr Fielding. But Frenchie's had plenty of time to think since he's been in my cage, an' I reckon he's talkin' straight. I've tol' Frenchie the judge won't listen to what he says to Mrs Fielding, but Frenchie still wants to go ahead.'

Fielding blew out through pursed lips. 'OK, Mrs Fielding's in the back store, I'll go an' have a word. If she agrees, we'll come to your office.'

'If she does agree I think it better if your wife comes with me.'

Fielding screwed up his mouth. 'Yeah, mebbe you're right. I'll go see her. No sayin' what I'd do if I see that sonovabitch agin.'

Harding waited a minute or so before Fielding and his wife came into the store. Mrs Fielding was taking off her dusty apron as she spoke to her husband. 'The Good Lord said we should forgive those who trespass against us, Benjamin. If this man wishes to say sorry, I should listen to him.'

Fielding shrugged his shoulders, seemingly resigned to his wife's intentions.

'That's mighty generous of you, Mrs Fielding,' Harding said. 'If you'll come with me, you'll be back with your husband in ten minutes or so.'

Harding escorted Mrs Fielding along the boardwalk and entered the office where Charlie had Frenchie standing a few feet in front of the door which led to the cages.

'Say what you've gotta say, Frenchie,' ordered Harding.

Frenchie looked at the storekeeper's wife for a few seconds and then lowered his eyes to stare at the floor. 'Mrs Fielding, I know you can't forgive me for what I did that night, but I just wanna say how sorry I am. I've never done anything like that to a real lady before, an' I swear I'll never do anythin' like that agin.' Frenchie raised his head, remorse showing in his eyes. 'I'm real sorry, ma'am.'

For several seconds there was total silence in the office. Then Mrs Fielding spoke. 'Everyone calls you Frenchie. You must have a proper name. What is it?'

'Paul Dupont, ma'am'

'Are you from the south, Mr Dupont?'

'No, ma'am. My kinfolk settled in a place called Quebec up north. I came south to soldier for the Union.'

Mrs Fielding studied him for a few moments. 'Mr Dupont, I forgive you.'

Frenchie raised his head. 'Thank you, ma'am.'

'Take him back, Charlie.'

The deputy put a hand on Frenchie who turned wordlessly and allowed himself to be guided back into the passageway leading to the cages.

'That's very generous of you, Mrs Fielding. I'll see you back to the store.'

'Thank you, Sheriff, I'd like that.'

'I'll just have a word with my deputy.' Harding turned back as Charlie re-appeared. 'I'm out for a while, Charlie. You OK with that?'

'Sure. I reckon it'll be quiet for a while after that Caxton business.'

'You could be right. I'll be back as soon as I can.'

Harding walked Mrs Fielding back to the store, made a small purchase, and five minutes later was hitching his roan in front of Amy's house. Felix greeted him as a regular visitor and he was shown into the parlour where he and Amy had met the day before. Ignoring propriety he strode across the room to sit beside her on the davenport.

'Have you been able to read Dale's shorthand?'

She didn't answer immediately, appearing to be deciding how she would respond. Finally she spoke. 'I'll tell you what I've found if you give me your word we'll share the reward if we find any gold.' She looked away from him, her face pink.

'I need that money, Clay. You may think that Mother and I are well placed here. We have some money, it's true, but life has not been easy for us since Father died. We've no men to look after us since my brothers died at Gettysburg and life has sometimes been hard.'

She looked back at him, her face blushing with embarrassment.

'Mother's jewellery. . . .' Her voice trailed away, and she looked down as if ashamed to look Harding in the eye.

'I'll do better than that,' he said, taking her hand. 'If we find the gold the reward is yours. As an Army officer I couldn't claim a share. Now tell me where the gold is hidden.'

Amy shook her head. 'I can't. Mr Dale doesn't mention any gold.'

Harding swore inwardly. 'What does Dale say?'

'He writes only of a wall of rock with a hole near the ground just big enough for a man to crawl through.'

Harding sat up suddenly. 'There's a wall of rock in the tunnel on the homestead Brenton sold to Pierce. I've been in it.' For an instant he had a mental picture of what he'd seen when he'd reached the end of the tunnel. 'And there was a hole near the ground.'

'Big enough for me to crawl through?'

'Yes, I reckon. But why ask that?'

'Mr Dale was a very small man, about my size. He could have crawled through the hole and found the gold,' she said, her eyes sparkling with excitement.

Harding's mouth set firm. 'Then why doesn't the Englishman refer to it in his journal? He may have found the eagle cockade behind the rocks but there's nothing to say he found Army gold.'

'Clay, we'll go and look! I could get through the rock and see if the gold is there!'

How had he known that she would want to take a look at the tunnel? But even he hadn't thought she'd suggest going through the rock wall. The idea was crazy.

'There's a long ladder to climb. Even in a riding skirt you'd probably fall.'

'But if I don't go with you how can I claim the reward?'

'I'll tell the Army you were with me.'

'You'd tell lies to your fellow officers?'

Harding hesitated. 'No, I couldn't do that,' he said finally.

'Then we go together!' Amy said triumphantly.

'Supposing Pierce finds us out there?'

'It's a risk we take.'

'This is crazy!' he said curtly, not bothering with his manners. He saw the determined look on her face and knew he would be unable to dissuade her from what she was proposing to do. 'But if you're going to insist, wait there.'

He jumped up from the davenport and strode out of the room, along the corridor, and out to his horse. He pulled from his saddle-bag the bundle he'd bought from Fielding and marched back into the house. He admired Amy's spirit but there were limits to what a man could expect from a gentlewoman, he decided. Maybe what he was carrying would convince her how foolishly she was acting. She appeared totally ignorant of the dangers. Apart from the ladder and the tunnel itself, if Pierce caught them on his land he would have no mercy.

He ignored Felix who stood outside the parlour, seemingly disturbed by the raised voices. Amy remained seated on the davenport, her expression clearly showing that she was puzzled by Harding's sudden exit and equally prompt reappearance.

'Here you are,' he said, handing her the bundle. 'If you are determined to go with me you'll have to wear these.'

As she took the bundle from him it unravelled and fell across her lap. She gave a shriek of dismay as the pair of denim work pants fell to the floor.

'I can't wear these!' She gave him a piercing glare. 'How did you ever think a lady would be seen in such a garment, showing her legs to every man who saw her?'

'I guess you're right. I'll get Charlie to help me. His kinfolk don't have too many worldly goods.'

'Clay Harding, you are not being a gentleman,' she snapped. 'Talk of your getting Mr Wilson to help is most unfair.' There was a moment's silence while they stared hard at each other. Then Amy's expression softened. 'Would you be the only man to see me?'

'I reckon so.'

'Then I'll do it. Mother's taking her nap so she'll not see.' Amy jumped to her feet, holding the denim pants. 'Wait here, Clay. I need to speak to Felix, and I'll tell Baskins you'll look after the horses.'

Without waiting for Harding's response she quickly left the room. He sat there turning over in his mind whether he was planning to do something very foolish. What if Pierce did find them searching the tunnel on property that now lawfully belonged to him? Even if Pierce and his men didn't catch up with them there was the risk of an accident. If Amy fell from the ladder he would never forgive himself.

He tried not to think about what would happen out at the old homestead, and to divert his mind he leafed through one of the books on a nearby shelf. After ten minutes the door behind him was opened and quickly shut. He put down the book and turned to see Amy dressed in the denim pants. She wasn't the first woman he'd seen without her skirts, not by far, but Amy Dawson, he decided, was a picture to raise a man's spirits and warm his heart.

'You're not to look at me like that!' Amy said, her face pink.

'I'll try not to,' Harding said. 'But it'll be tough. C'mon, before your mother finishes her nap.'

In less than an hour they reached the tunnel that stood on land previously owned by Bosun Brenton. For the whole of the ride Harding had kept a sharp lookout for any riders who might prove to be Pierce's men. But nothing caused him alarm. It was a little past noon and he remembered that Beth had told him that the no-goods who worked for Pierce took their main meal at midday.

He reined in his roan and swung down from the saddle. Despite her wearing pants and admitting she could ride across the horse Amy had kept to her side-saddle rather than alert Baskins to any change in her plans. She stepped down to the ground and secured her grey to a nearby fence post.

'What if our horses are seen?'

'We must hope they're not,' Harding said, as they stood at the entrance to the tunnel. He lit one of the two lamps he was carrying. 'Are you sure you want to go on with this?'

She nodded. 'I'll climb down after you. If I slip you can catch me.'

You'll probably kill us both, Harding thought. 'That's fine,' he said. He stepped from the timbers around the opening on to the ladder. 'I'll go down a few feet and then wait for you to step on to the ladder.'

He was more confident than his previous climb, knowing the wood of the ladder was strong enough to bear his weight. Being so much lighter, Amy would have no problem providing she kept her footing. If she did slip and fall on him he had to hope that her weight wouldn't wrench his hold away from the ladder, and that somehow she could regain her footing.

'Are you OK?' he called after he'd descended several feet.

'Yes, Clay,' came her reply, her voice quavering a little.

Slowly and carefully they descended the long ladder until finally the light from Harding's lamp showed that he was only two or three feet from the firm ground of the first chamber. Stepping from the bottom rung he stood back to assist Amy for the last couple of feet. She let out a deep sigh of relief.

'I thought the ladder would never end.' She looked around her. 'Are we here?'

Harding pointed to the shadowy opening on the far side of the chamber. 'We have to go through there. I'll go first.'

Amy breathed in deeply. 'I'll hold your belt.'

Together, Amy's hand on the back of Harding's gun-belt, they edged their way through the tunnel. As on his previous visit, Harding felt the strain on his leg muscles but thought it worthwhile when Amy threw both arms around his waist at the sounds of scampering feet and high-pitched squeaks of rats scurrying out of their way as they advanced. At last they reached the second cave and Harding held his lamp forward.

'There's the hole in the wall,' he said pointing. 'That could be the one the Englishman found.'

They approached the hole, both of them dropping to their knees to see if the light from Harding's lamp showed anything behind the wall of rocks. 'If the gold is behind these rocks the renegade soldiers must have used black powder to bring down the end of the tunnel the miners had dug,' Harding said. 'They probably planned to wait a while and then use powder again to reach the gold.'

'But wouldn't people in Jackson have heard the explosions?'

'Remember, we're talking thirty years ago, there weren't that many folks in these parts, and this was all open range.'

'I'm going through that hole,' Amy said determinedly.

Harding knew he'd reached the time to make a decision. He'd played along with Amy so far. If the gold was eventually found behind the rock she could lawfully claim that she'd found it and he would back her. But what would happen if she managed to get through and couldn't get back? She'd be trapped there until he could find a way of blasting the rock, and that could take days if not weeks.

'The schoolmarm could find a young boy with spirit to go in there. You don't have to do this.'

'I've said I'm going through and I shall.'

In the yellow light thrown from the single lamp he could

see the determined expression on her face. It was an expression he'd seen on some women driving the Conestoga wagons heading west to a new life.

'I'll light the other lamp,' he said. 'Push it ahead of you. Any rats will soon make a run for it, and you'll be fine.' They both stood up, and on an impulse he put his arm around her shoulders. 'I'm saying it again. You don't have to do this.'

She looked up at him, and smiled. 'Yes, I do,' she said. 'Light the lamp.'

He lit the lamp and placed it at the entrance to the hole. Amy lay flat on the ground and began to edge herself forward, pushing the lamp ahead until her head and shoulders entered the hole.

'Can you do it?' Harding asked, trying to keep the strain from his voice.

'I think so.'

Her voice was muffled, but strong, and Harding realized that she was going to be able to get through and reach the other side of the rock face. Inch by inch the soles of her boots edged away from him. He, too, was now lying flat on the ground watching her slow progress. As the light ahead began to fade, throwing her boots into shadow, her feet suddenly began to wriggle. He sucked in air, his muscles tightening but then he realized she must have reached the other side and was shifting her legs in order to stand. The light at the end of the opening disappeared and the hole in the rock wall went black.

'Can you see anything?' he called.

A shriek of triumph echoed along the tunnel and Harding guessed that she'd found something. But was it the gold? He felt like shouting a dozen questions but instead he scrambled to his knees, anxiously awaiting the sight of Amy's lamp reappearing at the end of the hole. There! The lamp shone and behind it Amy appeared, her face streaked with dirt as she pushed her way towards him.

He waited, willing her to squeeze her way through the narrow gap until finally she pushed the lamp into the cave where he crouched. Holding both her hands he gently hauled her the last few feet until she was clear of the hole. She rolled on to her back, and Harding was taken aback to see tears running down her cheeks. Anxiously, he dropped to one knee beside her.

'What's wrong? Are you hurt?'

'Oh, Clay! I'm so happy,' she said, the tears streaming down, creating rivulets among the dirt. 'I've found the gold! I'll be able to make up to Mother all her sacrifices she's made these last ten years.'

She held up her hand. In her clenched fist was a rag of dark blue, and what Harding guessed was the edge of a gold stripe. 'Three strongboxes, Clay!' She wriggled into a sitting position. 'I know they're Army strongboxes, I saw similar ones when I went with Mother to Fort Laramie.' She looked up at Harding. 'Will you send to Cheyenne for soldiers?'

'Don't worry about that now.' Taking her hands, Harding pulled Amy to her feet. 'There's nothing more we can do here,' he said.

'Do you think Pierce knows the gold is here?'

Harding had a mental flash of seeing Old Zack's hand settled on the rough blanket like a fatally wounded animal. 'I think he has some notion but maybe he doesn't know it's behind these rocks. C'mon, we'd best get back to town afore Pierce or his men appear.'

'You've been gone some while, Sheriff. Everythin' OK?'

Harding smiled broadly at his deputy, patted the head of Bruno who responded with a barely open eye, sniffed at Harding's pants leg, and promptly went back to sleep.

Harding poured himself coffee and walked across to take his seat behind the desk.

'Charlie,' he announced. 'We've found the stolen Army gold.'

Charlie's jaw dropped. 'Jumpin' rattlesnakes! Where in tarnation did you find it?'

Briefly, Harding described how Amy had been able to read the Englishman's journal and their subsequent ride out to the old coal tunnel where they'd both been a couple of days before.

'I remember you tellin' me about that hole. You sayin' Miss Dawson crawled through it?'

'That she did. Without her I still wouldn't know the whereabouts of the gold.'

The deputy looked thoughtful. 'I reckon Pierce knows about the gold. That's why Mather tortured poor Old Zack.'

'That's about it, Charlie.'

'So what do we do now? Send to Cheyenne for soldiers, I guess.'

Harding breathed in deeply. Now that his deputy knew where the gold was hidden would he go along with what he, Harding, was about to suggest? Charlie was right, of course. The obvious next move was to send for soldiers who would blast the rock face and recover the gold. To hell with it! He'd come this far, and there was no turning back.

'No, Charlie,' he said. 'We're gonna recover the gold ourselves.'

'Mr Harding, with all respect, we ain't able to get through that rock if it's like you said. We need a feller who knows about such things.'

'You're right. An' we've got one.' Harding pointed a thumb in the direction of the door to the cages. 'Frenchie,' he said.

CHAPTER TWELVE

Both men argued back and forward for almost half an hour. Harding was reluctant to order his deputy to do what he was told because deep down he knew Charlie had right on his side. The right move now was to send for help from Cheyenne but if he did that there was a real chance that the reward would slip away from Amy. He wasn't forgetting, too, that finding the gold without help from Cheyenne would strengthen his own position.

'Frenchie's our lawful prisoner,' Charlie said for the third or fourth time. 'We can't let him out of the cage to go minin'.'

'Pierce has a damned good notion of where that gold is. We wait for the soldiers and he could reach it before us.'

'But he'd need a miner.'

'How do you know he hasn't already sent for one? He sprung Caxton on us in a coupla days.'

Charlie chewed at his lip. 'Supposin' Frenchie can't do the job?'

'Then we have to send for the soldiers. If Pierce gets to the gold afore they arrive we'll think again.'

There was silence in the office while Charlie was clearly turning over in his mind what Harding had said. Finally he nodded. 'OK, you're the sheriff. I wouldn't be here talkin'' like this if you hadn't give me a chance.'

'Frenchie's horse is with Parkes at the livery. My roan will be back there too by now. Have both horses at the back of the clapboard, same as we did with Beth Pierce.'

'OK. C'mon, Bruno.'

At the sound of its name the bloodhound scrambled to its feet and followed Charlie out of the office. Harding sat still for several minutes thinking through what he was going to say to Frenchie. Then he stood up and went through to the cage carrying the jailhouse keys.

Frenchie looked up from reading the *Clarion*, which must have been brought in by Seb Haines. He looked up as Harding selected a large key and unlocked the cage door.

'We're gonna have a talk, Frenchie. But we'll talk in the office.'

Looking slightly bewildered by this unexpected turn of events Frenchie put down the paper on his bunk and got to his feet. Harding gestured that he should go ahead into the office, before resting his hand on the butt of his Colt. Frenchie looked more puzzled than dangerous but there was no point in taking chances.

'Take the seat in front of the desk,' Harding ordered. 'You want coffee?'

'Coffee would be good.'

Harding filled a couple of mugs from the pot and brought the mugs across to the desk, placing one before Frenchie. He took his seat and stared hard at the prisoner.

'I'm told you were a miner,' he said.

Frenchie nodded. 'Ten years.'

'So how come you fell in with the bunch of no-goods 'cross the Lode?'

'I got into a fight with one of the mine bosses. Nobody would give me any work.'

'Can you use black powder?'

123

'Sure I can, an' I can use the new dynamite stuff.'

'Supposin' I said I needed to blast a hole big enough for two men to carry a heavy box from one side of a rock wall to the other. Could you do it?'

Frenchie thought for a moment. 'I'd have to take a look, see what I was up agin.'

'I don't make deals with prisoners, Frenchie, but you do this an' I'll make sure the judge knows.'

Frenchie scowled. 'You're makin' this sound too easy. Are you lookin' for somethin' the same as Pierce?'

Harding was silent for a moment. 'What d'you know about that?'

Frenchie shrugged. 'That sonovabitch Mather got sent for. He was gonna do a job that had something to do with what Pierce was after. That's all I know.'

'There's a rock wall in a coal tunnel on an old homestead. It's now owned by Pierce.'

Frenchie's expression hardened. 'Let's get this straight. I blast on Pierce's land an' you say sweet words to the judge. That's the deal you're offerin'?'

'Yeah, that's it.'

'You're goddamned crazy!' Frenchie jumped to his feet. 'I'll go back to the cage.'

'Sit down!' Harding half rose from his chair, his hand on the butt of his Colt. 'Sit down! I'm tellin' you, Frenchie! Sit down!'

Slowly, Frenchie lowered himself to the chair, his head down. 'Pierce will kill us both,' he muttered. 'You don't know what he can do to a man.'

Harding relaxed back on to his chair and took a deep breath. 'S'posin' he catches up with us out at the tunnel. You'll be OK. You tell him some story how I made you help me. He's gonna believe it 'cos he'll want to.'

'That badge ain't gonna save you.'

Harding smiled grimly. 'I'll take my chances.'

He turned his head as the door from the street opened. Doc Radman stood in the doorway. He hesitated when he saw who was sitting in front of the desk.

'How's the foot, Frenchie?' Radman asked.

'Fine, Doc. I'm walkin' OK, thanks to you.'

Harding picked up the bunch of keys from the desk and escorted Frenchie back to the cage. 'We'll make a move when I've talked with Doc Radman,' he said, leaving Frenchie sitting on his bunk deep in thought.

Radman was sitting in front of the desk, a beaming smile on his face, when Harding closed the door to the passageway behind him. 'You look cheerful, Doc,' he said.

'The Lord works in mysterious ways,' said Radman. 'Never was anything said more truly.' He leaned forward. 'Josh Wake is not yet ready to meet his Maker. I was expectin' to find he'd passed over last night. When I took a look at dawn, he was able to speak, an' his breathin' was normal.'

'That's fine doctorin'.'

Radman shook his head. 'I'd like to agree but I can't. It's a miracle, that's all.'

'When can I ask him questions?'

'Give old Josh some time, Sheriff! If ever a man's come back from the dead, it's Josh Wake.' He pursed his lips, thinking. 'Mebbe tomorrow, better the day after.'

A sudden thought came to Harding. 'Have you tol' folks about Mr Wake recovering?'

'Not yet. I've been busy lookin' at the blacksmith's boy.'

'Then don't tell anyone.'

Radman frowned. 'Why not? This town needs good news. God knows, we haven't had much these past months.'

'Doc, if it gets out Mr Wake can put a name to the no-good who attacked him his life will be in danger. Better you let it be known that Mr Wake is still expected to die soon.'

'Heck! I never thought o' that. OK, I'll not say a word.' Radman stood up. 'Sure is a fine day, Sheriff. I gotta feelin' Jackson Creek is gonna be OK.'

Let's hope you're right, Doc, Harding thought, as the doctor closed the door behind him. Harding pulled open the drawer of his desk and took out a box of thirty-sixes. Riding out to the tunnel again was risking Pierce and his men finding him and Frenchie underground. All Pierce would have to do was wait until they emerged and pick off both of them. The rattlesnake would claim he thought he'd found thieves on his land, and a jury made up of men making money from Pierce would free him. He went through to where Frenchie was waiting.

'OK, Frenchie. Let's go see what you can do.'

They rode out of town unseen by any of Pierce's men and took the trail leading to the old homesteads. Save for a couple of cowboys from Green Valley they saw no other riders. Another time Harding would have stopped the cowboys and asked after Beth Pierce, or Beth Maynard, he should say, recalling her remarks to Henry Yorke.

In less than an hour the two men reached the tunnel. They swung down from their saddles, both taking a long look back in the direction of Jackson. Nobody had followed them.

'We gonna leave our horses in the open?'

'I guess so.' Harding pointed to an abandoned sod shack some twenty yards from the opening to the tunnel. 'That should hide them from a rider comin' from the trail goin' east. We gotta hope Pierce don't take it in his mind to come out an' look at the land he's just bought.'

Frenchie pulled a mouth. 'He ain't one for looking at bunch and buffalo grass. He likes places like the saloon

126

when he can get his hands on the women.'

They secured their mounts to a nearby fence post and readied themselves to climb down the ladder. 'I'll carry the lantern,' Frenchie said. 'You go first. I ain't gonna fall, but you might, an' I don't want you comin' down on me.'

'For a feller I just let outa jail you sure got a mouth on you,' Harding said. 'But I guess you're right.'

He stepped off the timbers and on to the first rung of the ladder. He was more relaxed, having already climbed down the ladder on two previous occasions. Halfway down Harding grinned to himself as he heard Frenchie swear.

'Goddamned rats!'

They reached the bottom and Harding pointed out the next stage of the passage to the rock wall. Third time or not, Harding's knees still ached as he made his way along the narrow passage to the second chamber and he was glad when at last the tunnel roof above him began to slope upwards, allowing him to stretch to his full height. They both stepped into the second cave and Frenchie held the lantern above his head.

'Fer cris'sakes!' Frenchie exploded. 'What the hell happened here?'

'I'm guessin' the men who blasted this weren't sure what they were doin' and used too much powder.'

'I'm tellin' you now. I try an' blast through that an' I'm gonna have the goddamned river up to my neck.'

'Bring the lantern over here,' Harding said. He moved across the cave to stand near the hole which Amy Dawson had crawled through. Frenchie followed him and grunted as he saw the opening Harding was pointing at. Handing the lantern to Harding, Frenchie dropped to his knees to peer along the opening.

'A small man or a boy mebbe could get through there,' Frenchie said.

'Yeah, but he couldn't bring back what's behind the rock wall.'

Frenchie looked at him. 'You gonna tell me what that is?'

Harding hesitated. Should he tell Frenchie? If Pierce already knew what was hidden there was no harm in telling Frenchie. But he'd long since learned that men could go crazy when they heard that gold was there for the taking. Frenchie was going along with him so far, why risk him thinking he could gain more than words in his favour in front of the judge.

'Three strongboxes containing money.' He held up his hand as he saw the gleam appear in Frenchie's eyes. 'Don't get your pants on fire. It's Confederate money left over from the War.'

'Then it ain't worth two bits.'

Harding stared unblinking at Frenchie. He remembered the advice given to him when he had briefly worked in Washington. Mr Pinkerton, President Lincoln's spy chief, had told the assembled young officers, 'If you're gonna lie, gentlemen, lie big.'

'There's a passel o' Johnny Rebs who don't go along with that. They're gonna try to fight the War agin. They've stashes like this around the country. I've been sent from Cheyenne to find this one.'

'Pierce ain't from the South.'

'No, he ain't. But he'd take money from anyone ready to pay him.'

'The two-timin' sonovabitch!' Frenchie snarled. 'I'll make a list of what I need. That hole ain't gonna be any trouble.'

Harding pursed his lips in a silent whistle. 'OK, Frenchie. Let's get back to town.'

For the climb back up the ladder Frenchie said he'd go first, arguing that if Harding fell below him he'd certainly be killed and he, Frenchie, could then hightail it out of the territory. Harding glared at his prisoner and was surprised to see Frenchie grinning. Since being faced with a task that called on his old skills he appeared to be in a more pleasant frame of mind.

'Just joshin' you, Mr Harding. But I still reckon I should go first.'

'OK, you do that, an' you carry the lantern. An' afore you get too sassy remember you're goin' back to the jailhouse.'

With Frenchie a few rungs above him Harding began to make the climb. Again he found it much easier than before, and knowing that he'd be doing it again a couple of times he was glad that the strain on his muscles was beginning to ease.

Above him he was aware that Frenchie had reached the top and had stepped off the ladder. Half a dozen rungs later Harding thrust his head and shoulders above the opening to the tunnel. Then he froze for an instant before his hand dropped to the butt of his Colt.

'Jesse's gotta Winchester aimed at your head, Harding! He ain't gonna miss from ten feet,' called Pierce. A dozen riders were lined up either side of Pierce, the men watching him with mocking smiles on their unshaven faces. 'You get off that ladder, an' move real slow. That badge ain't gonna save you now you're trespassin' on a man's land.'

Harding didn't move, calculating the odds of dropping down the ladder out of sight but then, he reckoned, he'd be trapped underground and Pierce could take his time working out how he could finish him off.

'I ain't a patient man, Harding. Now do as you're god-damned told an' step outa there.' Pierce waited while Harding stepped from the ladder to the ground beside the tunnel. 'OK, now you drop that gun-belt, an' kick it away. You reach for that Colt o' yourn an' Jesse's gonna put one through your eye.'

Harding did as ordered. As long as he was alive he had a chance. There was no sense in making the wrong move. He had no doubt that the no-good Jesse would grab the chance to shoot him. As if to confirm his thoughts, Jesse called out.

'Why don't we just shoot the sonovabitch right now!'

'Shut your mouth Jesse, an' keep that long gun ready. We shoot a lawman an' we'll have fifty of his pardners riding from Cheyenne.' Pierce looked in turn at the lines of men either side of him. 'We're gonna do it different. Sheriff Harding's gonna have an accident.'

'Just like that crazy Englishman,' one of the riders called out, and a raucous cheer went up. 'Let's do it now!'

'We'll do it when I say so,' Pierce barked. 'Put your long gun on Harding,' he ordered the rider alongside him. 'Jesse, you and Stein get down an' search Harding.'

The two men dismounted and approached Harding. Jesse drew his hands roughly down Harding's front. He pulled out the box of shells from Harding's trail jacket and the .22 pocket-gun from the inside pocket of Harding's vest, then feeling down Harding's legs, turned up the cuff of his pants, and pulled out the broad-bladed knife from the top of Harding's boot.

'You're a reg'lar general store, Harding,' Jesse leered. 'Now turn 'round.'

Harding did as he was ordered.

'Well, damnitall, Mister Sheriff! You sure ain't takin' no chances.' Jesse pulled the sheath from where it had been tucked in the top of Harding's pants. 'Hey, I know this knife! Ain't this yourn, Frenchie?'

'Hold it there, Jesse,' Pierce barked, as Jesse made to throw the sheathed knife across to Frenchie. 'I ain't finished with Frenchie.' He turned his head to stare for several seconds at Frenchie who stood unmoving the other side of the tunnel opening from Harding.

130

'How come you're helpin' the sheriff, Frenchie?'

'The sonovabitch said if I didn't help him blast out some rock he was gonna shoot me an' tell the judge I was tryin' to escape from jail.'

Pierce took several seconds to seemingly turn over in his mind what Frenchie had told him. Finally, he nodded.

'You seen where he wanted you to blast?'

'Yeah, I seen it. But, Mr Pierce, it ain't an easy job. I'm gonna have to study it for a few days or the tunnel's gonna get flooded.'

Harding's expression didn't change. Frenchie was talking fast to save his own skin. But what was the truth? Underground, he'd have sworn that Frenchie was telling the truth when he said there'd be no problem blasting the hole Amy had crawled through. Frenchie was playing for time, he decided, and planning to put Jackson Creek behind him as soon as he could.

'Blackie,' Pierce addressed one of the riders. 'Leave your horse an' we'll take it back to town. Take Harding's horse, an' ride with Frenchie to that cabin where Mather and Caxton hid up. You know where it is?'

'Sure, boss.'

'OK, Jesse. You can give Frenchie his knife.'

He waited while Jesse tossed over the sheathed knife. 'OK, Jesse, you an' Stein take Harding to Old Zack's cabin for a day or so while I work out how the sheriff's gonna have an accident.'

'Boss, we've only got two horses,' Jesse pointed out.

A malicious smile appeared on Pierce's face. 'Then the sonovabitch is gonna have to walk.'

Pierce turned his horse's head back in the direction of Jackson Creek and kicked it into a gallop, his men falling in line behind him.

*

131

No man went afoot in Wyoming, Harding told himself, as he stumbled along, desperately trying to stay upright at the end of the rope secured to Jesse's saddle. The rope binding his wrists together rubbed off the skin as it drew taut. He quickened his pace, ungainly in his heeled boots. Whatever happened he knew he had to keep to his feet or Jesse, he guessed, would drag him all the way to Old Zack's cabin. Every so often Jesse would look behind him and with a leer would nudge his mount into a quicker pace forcing Harding into a trot in order to keep the rope slack. But finally, as Harding was beginning to think he could walk no longer, they reached the dirt track to the cabin once occupied by Old Zack.

'Hey, Jesse, there's blood on this track,' called Stein, a few yards ahead.

'Drop o' blood ain't gonna hurt you,' shouted Jesse, but his hand dropped to the butt of his sidearm. 'Make sure no passin' drifter ain't holed up in there.'

His sidearm drawn, Stein swung down from his saddle, and cautiously pushed open the door. He stood for a moment in the doorway before turning back to where Jesse had halted his mount. Harding sucked in air, mindful that he hadn't covered so much ground on foot since he'd been at law school.

'It's OK, Jesse, place is empty,' Stein called.

Jesse swung down to the ground. He unhitched the rope from his saddle, and heaved on it, forcing Harding to follow him, as he entered the cabin.

'Hell! What went on here?' Jesse said, staring down at the bloodstains on the floor. He looked around. 'But it looks OK.' He tugged on the rope as he crossed to the large wooden box that stood in the corner, peering in the open top. 'Plenty o' fixin's here. We ain't gonna starve fer a coupla days.'

He jerked the rope suddenly, almost pulling Harding off his feet.

'We'll tie this sonovabitch's hands behind his back. He's gonna be no trouble.'

Stein grunted. 'We gonna be here that long? How about when he goes out to the privy? I ain't gonna hold it for him.'

Jesse looked around the cabin. 'I got an idea.' He took out his sidearm and placed it on the table. Then he heaved on the rope, and crossed the cabin to the wall opposite the pot-bellied stove, pulling Harding behind him.

'I'm gonna take the rope off your wrists, Harding. You make a wrong move an' Stein's gonna shoot you.'

'You know you're gonna hang for this, Jesse,' Harding said.

'Yeah, guess I will,' Jesse said. 'Only you ain't gonna be here to see it.'

Jesse untied the ropes, and immediately stepped back. He looked to his right. 'You see that picture over there?'

'I see it.'

'You come past that line, and you're gonna get shot. That's your deadline, you unn'erstand?'

'Yeah. Can I have some water?'

'You'll get water when me an' Stein gets it.'

Harding nodded. With his back against the cabin wall he allowed himself to slide down until he was seated on the floor, glad to give his aching feet a rest. The blisters on his feet were painful but it was no good his mind dwelling on such trivial matters when almost certainly he would be dead within a couple of days. He had one card in his hand but with two men watching him he was unable to see how he could play it. He'd maybe take one of the no-goods with him but the other would shoot him down. He'd thought there was irony in the death of Frank Warden, but how much more would there be if he, too, met his end in a small town

like Jackson. Would Amy mourn him for long? Maybe the
cattle-dealer in Chicago she'd told him about would come
courting again.

'You gonna get some water, Stein?' Jesse sat by the table,
checking over his sidearm.

'Why the hell don't you get water?' Stein said peevishly.

'Cos, I'm gonna rustle up some grub, that's why,' Jesse
barked. 'Now do as I say.'

Muttering beneath his breath, Stein walked across to pick
up the bucket and head on outside.

Jesse looked across at Harding. 'Don't think o' doin'
anythin' stupid 'cos Stein's gone out.'

'I ain't gonna—'

Harding's reply was cut off by the crack of a long gun. For
a moment there was silence in the cabin and then Jesse
jumped to his feet. He rushed to the door, opening it a
crack.

'Christ! Some sonovabitch has shot Stein.'

Jesse spun around, his sidearm coming up to aim at
Harding. But he was too late. Harding's slim throwing knife,
pulled from the sheath at the nape of his neck, sank inches
into Jesse's fleshy throat. Blood spurted to widen the stains
already on the floor. A gurgling sound came from Jesse as he
plucked ineffectively at the handle of the knife and then he fell
face down, his whole body quivering before becoming still.

Harding jumped to his feet, and strode across the cabin
to snatch up his own gun-belt and the box of shells Jesse had
placed on the table. He buckled on the belt and moved cautiously to the door, opening it no more than an inch. He
could see the inert body of Stein on the ground, the empty
bucket a few yards away. Who was out there? Should he call
out or was it best to wait for the shootist to show himself?

Then he heard a sound. Surely that was a dog's bark.
Christ! Bruno was out there, and that surely meant Charlie.

He opened the cabin door another inch or two.

'Charlie Wilson!' Harding shouted. 'Is that you out there?'

A mounted figure broke from the nearby stand of cottonwoods, Bruno running around in circles behind him. 'OK, Mr Harding!' Charlie shouted. 'Tol' you Bruno was gonna do fine.'

Harding recovered his knife, wiping the blade on Jesse's shirt before slipping it back into its sheath below his shirt. He stood at the doorway, his Colt down by his pants leg, as Charlie reined in and swung down from his saddle. He walked over to Harding, and thumped him on the shoulder, apparently elated that he'd come to the rescue.

'We did it, Mr Harding! Me an' Bruno! We did it!'

'An' I'm damned glad you did, Charlie. But how did you know how to find me?'

'When you an' Frenchie didn't come back I thought you might be at Miss Dawson's so I called on her. She tol' me she hadn't seen you but you could be at Bosun's old place.'

'Yeah, I was. But how did you get here?'

'I got to the tunnel, an' Bruno went crazy, barkin' an' runnin' around, his nose on the ground. I reckoned he was on to somethin' and just followed him. Then I guessed he'd picked up your scent.' Charlie stopped and frowned. 'But now I come to think about it, how did he do that?'

Harding grinned, thankful for every blister on his feet. 'I was afoot, Charlie. Pierce made me walk here. That's how Bruno picked up my scent.'

Charlie slapped his thigh with delight. 'Jumpin' rattlesnakes! How's about that!' His expression changed suddenly, his mouth setting in a grim line. 'What we gonna do now, Mr Harding?'

Harding blew out air. 'We're gonna put Pierce behind bars, Charlie, an' if we can't do that we'll kill the sonovabitch.'

CHAPTER THIRTEEN

Night was beginning to cast its shadows as Harding and Charlie reined in a quarter of a mile from Main Street. Both men had remained silent since riding from Old Zack's cabin, both occupied with their thoughts of what lay ahead.

Harding, riding the horse which had belonged to the dead Jesse, had been puzzling over how to corner Pierce. The saloon owner had too many men backing him for the small force that Harding could muster. He was confident the Navy men would back him, and maybe one or two of the ex-soldiers around the town would stand, but the forces of law would still be overwhelmed. With no clear solution he decided to put aside the problem until later. But there were some actions he could take straight away, he decided.

'I'm gonna keep outa sight, and ride back o' the stores to my clapboard,' Harding told Charlie. 'You ride down Main Street, then get hold of Seb Haines. Give him a dollar an' tell him to take a coupla drinks in the Lode.'

Charlie was quick to see what Harding was about. 'Seb spreads the story that I can't find you.'

'That's it. After you've seen Seb go see Bosun Brenton an' ask him to come to the clapboard. I'm hopin' the Navy men will back us if it comes to a shoot-out.'

'They're good men,' Charlie said. 'I reckon they'll stand.'

136

'OK, Charlie, get some sleep tonight. Tomorrow's gonna be a big day.'

'I'll bunk down in one of the cages,' Charlie said, turning his mount's head in the direction of Main Street.

The town was dark save for a couple of lamps and the splash of light thrown from the saloon. Harding had no trouble reaching his clapboard without being seen. He swung down from the saddle and with his Colt in his hand, pushed open the rear door. Nothing stirred; satisfied the place was empty, he holstered his sidearm and crossed to close the shutters overlooking the street. Taking a match from his vest pocket he lit the lamp. If any of Pierce's men caught a glimpse of light they'd put it down to Charlie. He looked around. As usual the place was spotless. He remembered what Amy had said about training Lucy to be a housemaid. The young girl deserved to better herself.

He opened the cupboard where he knew Lucy always kept food in case he felt disinclined to walk down to the Chinaman. That was when he heard the gentle tap on the rear door. Charlie must have found Seb quickly and alerted Brenton. But caution had kept him alive and he pulled out his Colt before he opened the door.

'Frenchie! What the hell?'

Harding took a pace back, his left hand steadying Frenchie as the big man tottered forward. Quickly, Harding closed the door, pushing his Colt back in its holster and helping Frenchie to a chair. In the yellow light of the lamp, he saw the blood covering Frenchie's shirt at the shoulder and the rough packing around his neck. Harding reached down to a shelf where he kept a bottle below a couple of spare shirts.

'Here, take some of this.'

Frenchie took the bottle, pulling out the cork, and taking a long swig of the whiskey. 'Sonovabitch Blackie tried to kill me, winged me in my neck. I didn't want to kill him but it was him or me.'

'How the hell did that happen?'

'I tried to tell him we was doin' things wrong, goin' along with Pierce, an' we should quit now an' he should get outa the Territory.'

'An' what were you gonna do?'

'What I'm doin' now. I ain't ridin' the owl-hoot trail for the rest o' my life. I'll do my time down in Cheyenne an' start agin.'

'I got some biscuits and stuff. You hungry?'

'I ain't eaten all day.'

'OK, sit there an' take it easy.'

Harding was heating water for coffee when an idea occurred to him. If Frenchie was willing to risk his life there might be a way to scare some of the no-goods into quitting. His small force might then be strong enough to take them on. Pierce could yet end up in one of the cages. Or face down in the dirt of Main Street.

'Did Blackie tell you how many men Pierce has with him?'

'Mebbe thirty. But a dozen or so have only come into town these last coupla days. Blackie said Pierce had offered them big money. There was even talk of gold, but I reckon that was just Pierce talkin'.'

Harding's expression didn't change. He poured them both coffee and pushed the biscuits across the table. He looked at Frenchie thoughtfully. Would he be prepared to risk his life to clean the slate?

'Frenchie, you do somethin' for me an' I'm gonna let you go free. Don't worry about Ben Fielding. You help bring down Pierce an' he'll give you the run of his store.'

'You set me free an' I'll work for Fielding this winter fer nothin'.' Frenchie said. 'But I guess from what you're gonna say I might not be around.'

'You gotta choose.'

Frenchie stared down at the table, silent for a few moments. 'Whatever you're thinkin' on, I gotta have an even chance o' comin' out alive,' he said, looking up at Harding. 'What you want me to do?'

'You go back to the Lode. Tell 'em a coupla dozen soldiers are ready to ride in tomorrow lookin' to even the score for Frank Warden, an' they ain't takin' prisoners.'

'How am I s'posed to know that?'

'Tell 'em Caxton turned up at the cabin, his three nogoods havin' left him when they ran into soldiers.' Harding thought for a moment. 'Caxton shot you by mistake, thinkin' he was gonna take over the cabin from some drifter.'

'So where's Caxton and Blackie s'posed to be now?'

'They've hightailed it south. You've come back to warn your old pardners about the soldiers.'

Frenchie bit into a biscuit. 'You sure make some tough deals. You reckon Pierce is just gonna let me walk away tomorrow?'

'Tomorrow Pierce is gonna be dead.'

'Mr Harding, you sound mighty sure o' yourself. How d'you know it ain't gonna be me, you an' that kid deputy o' yourn headin' for Boot Hill?'

'I don't,' admitted Harding, 'but Pierce has driven decent folks away from this town. He was aimin' to kill me an' make it look an accident. He had Mather torture Old Zack which killed the old man, and he attacked Josh Wake. The time has come to settle accounts.'

Frenchie got to his feet, steadier now he'd had food and coffee. 'I got your word you'll square me with Mr Fielding?'

'You've got my word, Frenchie,' Harding said, also standing. He thrust out his hand. 'Good luck.'

Frenchie shook his hand, nodded, and without a further

word went out of the clapboard.

After retrieving his Winchester from the scabbard on his roan, Harding spent the next hour cleaning his long gun and his Colt. If he was going to survive the following day there must be no chance that either weapon would misfire. He was taking a box of Winchester ammunition from a leather case to put it alongside the box of thirty-sixes when he heard the tap on the door. He held his Colt ready as he opened it.

'C'mon in, Bosun, an' you too, Charlie. Drop of fine whiskey here for you both while we talk.'

The three men sat at the table, sipping their whiskey while Harding, having received Brenton's assurances that all the Navy men would stand with him, outlined his plan for the following day.

'If all those no-goods stay with Pierce,' Harding explained, 'we're gonna have to think agin. We get shot up an' Pierce will do what he fancies with the town.'

'But we can't go in the Lode after them,' Charlie said.

'You're damned right,' Harding said. 'D'you know where Pierce's men sleep at night?'

'Mebbe a few with the calico queens, most of 'em in a sorta bunkroom at the back o' the saloon. There's a door leading into it on the right of the little platform for the fiddlers an' the pianna player.'

'Any back way outa the bunkroom?'

'No.'

Harding turned to Brenton. 'Your men got their long guns ready for use?'

Brenton smiled grimly. 'We're gunners. They're always ready.'

Harding breathed in deeply. 'OK, this is what we're gonna do.'

He spent the next half hour or so explaining what he

wanted from Bosun's men, and what he and Charlie intended to do. After answering a few questions, he was satisfied that they both understood.

'Charlie, there's one last thing. Frenchie's across in the saloon an' I've made a deal with him.'

The deputy's eyebrows shot up. 'You said he'd been taken off to some cabin.'

'He came back an' he's across in the Lode tellin' those no-goods there's a bunch of soldiers heading this way intent on killin' every man jack as revenge for Frank Warden's death.'

'Then why ain't we waitin' for the soldiers?'

'Cos they don't exist. I'm hopin' a bunch o' no-goods will take to the hills. Gives us a better chance o' takin' Pierce. Frenchie's put his life on the line. He gets to walk free is the deal.'

Charlie nodded slowly. 'OK,' he said slowly. He opened his mouth to add something but appeared to change his mind and said nothing.

'Thanks for comin', Bosun. We'll see you tomorrow.'

Brenton left and Harding poured more whiskey into Charlie's glass and then into his own. They silently raised their glasses to each other in salute.

'You know where the gold is?' Harding asked.

'Bosun's old homestead, behind the rock wall.'

'You know Frenchie can blast through the hole? Bosun an' his men could get it to the surface.'

'Sure, an' if Frenchie can't handle it the soldiers from Cheyenne have to be told.'

'An' you know Miss Dawson found the gold?'

'Sure, I do.' Charlie frowned. 'Why we goin' through all this now?'

'If I don't make it, you'll be the only one on the right side of the law who knows about the gold an' who found it.'

141

'Fer cris'sakes, Mr Harding!'

Harding smiled grimly. 'I ain't plannin' to cash in my chips just yet, Charlie. But I want to know if anythin' happens to me, Miss Dawson will get the reward for findin' the gold.'

Charlie's mouth set in a hard line. 'I'll see to it, Mr Harding.'

CHAPTER FOURTEEN

Harding rolled out of his bunk as dawn was breaking. He washed his hands and face in cold water from the tin bowl and sucked greedily at the cold coffee standing in the pot from overnight. He checked his Colt, picked up his Winchester, settled his hat, and was ready for the day. He pushed open the rear door of the clapboard to see Charlie leaning against the timbers of the sheriff's office.

'Mornin', Mr Harding.'

Charlie pulled at the brim of his hat, and Harding couldn't resist a smile. The stranger he'd chosen to be his deputy on the first day he'd arrived in the town had proved to be a fine young man. Putting Pierce behind bars was only half the job; he had to keep Charlie alive.

'We'll go down back of the stores until we're opposite the Lode,' Harding said. 'The big horse trough will keep us outa the way when the lead starts flyin'.'

Both men walked quickly along the back of the stores until they reached the livery, where they went around the side of the building, walked through the alleyway to Main Street and ducked down behind the water trough.

'Long guns,' ordered Harding. 'We ain't gonna hit anythin' at this range with sidearms.'

Charlie took a quick look across the street. 'Pablo's come

out. He's gonna brush down the boardwalk.'

Harding waited. He looked at his deputy. 'You ready for this?'

Charlie nodded. 'Ready.'

'Pablo!' Harding called. 'You hear me?'

There was a pause and Harding guessed the Mexican barkeep was trying to work out where the call had come from. '*Sí sí*, I hear you! Who is that calling?'

'Any o' those no-goods ridin' last night?'

'*Sí*, Mr Harding.' Pablo sounded more at ease now he'd realized who was calling across the street. 'Frenchie came in, an' after ten men ride out.'

'Listen, Pablo. You go back in there, tell those no-goods we're gonna jail 'em. You get under your bar an' stay there until this is over.'

There was a pause and Charlie took a quick look over the trough.

'Pablo's just cottoned on,' he said.

There was a yell from the Mexican and his straw broom went flying into the street. Nothing happened for several minutes. Then a rough voice rang out from inside the saloon.

'Harding! Nobody wants to die here but if you're spoilin' for a fight we're ready for it.'

'Bosun!' Harding shouted.

Two ropes snaked across the width of Main Street, grappling hooks at each end, which slammed around the wooden posts supporting the batwing doors to the saloon. Both ropes went bar straight and with a screaming of broken wood the whole of the entrance to the saloon was torn out and dragged back across Main Street.

'Jesus Christ!' Charlie exploded.

The words were barely out of his mouth when a dozen Winchesters on the roof of the store above where Harding and Charlie crouched rained lead through the entrance to the saloon. Two of the men inside let out agonized screams as they were hit.

'Reload!' Bosun shouted, and there came simultaneous ratcheting of a dozen or more Winchesters. 'Fire!'

'Sonovabitch!' Charlie swore. 'You ever seen anythin' like that!'

The riflemen had shifted their aim. Lead shattered the windows of the front of the saloon. As chips of wood sprayed through the air, and shards of glass glistened in the early morning light, the ropes were slackened to back release the grapnel hooks from the splintered wood, and hauled back across the street.

But Pierce's men were not going to give up easily. The street was suddenly full of the sounds of gunfire, lead flying across the street as both sides fought for the upper hand. A shout of pain from above Harding meant that one of the Navy men had been hit. As if in anger, the Navy men responded with a fusillade of shots that rained lead through the wrecked entrance to the saloon.

'Down, Brenton, down!' Harding yelled, and above him, bodies thudded on the roof. 'Fer cris'sakes,' Harding muttered to Charlie. 'I reckon they were standin' up!'

From the saloon came a volley of shots from long guns and sidearms. At least one man in the saloon had realized two men were behind the horse trough. Both Harding and Charlie winced as more slugs thudded into the wood of the trough, spraying water above their heads.

'Two men in the windows above!' Harding shouted.

He ducked around the side of the trough, raising his Winchester to aim at the windows above but was hampered by the swinging signboard of the saloon. Again two ropes snaked across the street, their grapnels hooking on to the signboard. A moment later the board was ripped from its supports giving Harding a clear view. A shadow moved in the window and Harding squeezed the trigger of his Winchester, reloading immediately to fire again. There was an agonized cry of pain, the window shattered, and a figure toppled forward to drop to the dirt of the street.

Harding risked a look above the trough and saw through the destroyed entrance a shadow move inside the saloon. Anticipating the movement he gently squeezed the trigger of his Winchester and heard the sound of tables crashing over as the no-good fell to the floor. But had he hit Pierce? It seemed unlikely that Pierce would put himself in the firing line. So where the hell was he?

'Bosun, you hear me?' Harding called.

'I hear you.'

'Hold your fire until I give the word.'

'I got that.'

'Your men OK?'

'One of 'em hit. But it ain't serious.'

Harding put down his Winchester, and cupped his hands around his mouth in the direction of the saloon. 'This is Sheriff Harding,' he shouted. 'You in the Lode. Can you hear me?'

'We hear you,' came a rough voice.

'The soldiers'll be here in a coupla hours. You all plannin' to die today?'

'You sonsovbitches,' came the defiant shout. 'Mebbe it's you critters gonna get killed.'

'I gotta deal fer you afore the soldiers get here. You wanna listen?'

A different voice called. 'We're listenin'.'

From inside the saloon came the sounds of angry voices. Harding guessed the men were arguing among themselves, some ready to listen to a deal, others ready to carry on fighting. There was a lull of several minutes. Then finally a voice called out.

'OK, what's the deal?'

Charlie looked at Harding. 'They're gonna go fer it!'

'I want Pierce an' Frenchie in the jailhouse. The rest o' you ride outa town.'

'Yeah, an' that crazy bunch o' bastards on the roof shoot us as we come out.'

'That's not gonna happen. I give you my word. Where are your horses?'

'Down at the livery.'

'They ain't gonna try an' break out at the back an' be afoot,' Charlie said.

'You're right. Take four o' Bosun's men an' get to the livery. Those no-goods are gonna go fer the deal, but we ain't takin' chances. They make any wrong move an' you shoot 'em down. Soon as they've left town get to the back of the Lode in case there's one of 'em wants to die a hero.'

'You reckon Pierce will let 'em walk out?'

Harding frowned. 'I'm thinkin' Pierce has already gone. I reckon we'd have heard from him by now.'

Charlie nodded, and, bent low, scuttled away into the alleyway out of the firing line of the men in the Lode. Harding remained on one knee, his Colt in hand, behind the trough. He'd be damned stupid if one of the no-goods was still intent on settling old scores.

'Bosun, you ready for this?'

'Ready, Mr Harding.'

'OK, you in the Lode,' Harding called. 'Come on out now. One of you makes a wrong move an' you'll all be shot down. You get your horses an' ride outa town. You think o' comin' back an' you'll be shot on sight. Frenchie an' Pierce stay there until I give 'em the word. You got that?'

'We got that,' one of the men shouted. 'We're comin' out now.'

147

Warily, Harding raised his head above the trough. Across the street from the shadows of the saloon men began to appear. Their heads down, they shuffled across the board-walk and down the steps to the hardpack of the street. Frenchie was not among them. Neither was Pierce.

Above Harding came the ratchet sounds of Winchesters being readied to fire, and the movement of boots as the Navy men moved to keep the group in their sights. Five minutes later the stand-off came to an end as the mounted men appeared from the livery, kicking their horses forward to ride out of town.

'Bosun, keep your men down,' he called. 'I'm gonna call Frenchie out if he's still alive. I reckon Pierce has gone but I ain't sure.' He swung around, still on one knee, his Colt at the ready. He had to reckon that one of the no-goods had remained and was ready to shoot anyone who walked into the saloon.

'Frenchie! You come out now!'

Nothing stirred. Had the ex-miner survived? Maybe Pierce had realized that Frenchie's story didn't stand up and had killed him. A shadow moved at the entrance. Then Harding saw Frenchie.

'Walk across the street to the water trough, Frenchie,' Harding called.

Frenchie stepped out of the saloon on to the boardwalk. Harding could see he was ashen-faced, sweat running down his unshaven cheeks. He made no move to step down on to the hardpack. What the hell was Frenchie waiting for?

'Fer cris'sakes, Frenchie! Get across here.'

At last Frenchie began a slow walk. He was halfway towards Harding when he stopped again. Harding swore. Was the neck wound slowing Frenchie down? He looked more terrified than in pain, standing unmoving in the middle of the street. Then another voice rang out from inside the saloon.

'That's far enough, Frenchie.'

Pierce! Harding recognized his voice immediately. Pierce was alone in the saloon, and had no chance of escaping. But what was this business with Frenchie? The ex-miner had done everything he'd been asked to do, and had earned his freedom. He opened his mouth to urge Frenchie on, but before he could do so, Pierce's voice rang out again.

'You can give that sonovabitch the message now, Frenchie.'

To Harding's surprise Frenchie took off like a scared jackrabbit, twisting and turning as he raced towards the horse trough. He flung himself to the hardpack alongside the trough, rolling along the dirt to gain shelter as shots rang out from the saloon, dirt kicking up alongside the trough.

'Bastard was gonna shoot me in the legs, so I could still speak,' Frenchie choked out. 'Pierce knows he's gonna go down, an' he aims to take you with him.'

'What the hell you talkin' about? An' why's Pierce talkin' about a message?'

'I gotta tell you. He's got Miss Dawson in there with him.'

An iron fist closed around Harding's heart, and his hand shot out to clutch at Frenchie's shirt. 'You're crazy! She's safe at home.'

'I've seen her, I tell ya! Pierce believed what I said about the soldiers comin' an' said we all had to stand an' fight. He knows he's finished but first he wants to kill you, Mr Harding, an' he reckons takin' Miss Dawson will give him his chance.'

'Has he harmed her in any way?'

Frenchie shook his head. 'He only took her an hour or so ago.'

'Bosun!' Harding shouted. 'You stay outa this. Miss

149

Dawson's in with Pierce an' I ain't takin' chances.'

'Sheriff, I don't think—'

'I tol' you, stay outa this!'

Brenton sounded subdued. 'OK, Mr Harding.'

Harding stood up from behind the trough, his Colt in its holster, his hands in view. 'You gonna hide behind a woman all your life, Pierce?' he shouted. 'Beth Maynard coulda swung fer what you did.'

Nothing stirred for a few moments. Harding's muscles across his back were as taut as wire. He stretched the fingers of his right hand. There was nothing to stop Pierce shooting him with a long gun from inside the saloon. He felt the jab of fear across his gut but he was gambling his life that Frenchie had got it right. Pierce wanted to kill him face to face.

'Don't you worry, Amy,' he shouted. 'I was faster than Mather an' I'm faster than Pierce!'

Would his deliberate boasts tempt Pierce to emerge from the saloon? Nothing moved for several moments. Then Harding got his answer. At the entrance to the saloon Amy appeared, being pushed forward, forced to shield the figure of Jake Pierce. Her face was chalk-white, tears staining her cheeks but her head was high. Slowly, the two figures stepped down to the hardpack.

'Let her go, Pierce. This is between you an' me.'

'I ain't finished yet!' Pierce yelled.

With a sweep of his arm he thrust Amy aside, sending her tumbling into the dirt, his sidearm already raised. Harding had a split second to see the red star of blood show on Pierce's forehead, jerking his head back, before the heavy slug from Pierce's sidearm slammed into his body, sending him reeling backwards into darkness.

CHAPTER FIFTEEN

Radman stared for several seconds at Harding. 'How's it feel now?'

'Aches like hell, Doc,' Harding said. He glanced down at the thick bandaging around his shoulder. 'This arm ever gonna be any use to me?'

'It'll take time but your Army days are over.' The doctor pulled up the corner of his mouth. 'Good thing you took the slug on your left side or you'd be real slow pullin' that Colt o' yourn.'

'Those days are over, Doc. I'm gonna be pushin' a pen from now on.'

'When's Charlie takin' over?'

'Tomorrow. Charlie's seein' the mayor now to get sworn in. Since the good folks of Jackson want him as sheriff he doesn't have to stand for election. I'm gonna stay around for a few days, then I'm takin' the stage to Cheyenne.'

'You gonna come back here?'

'There's nothin' for me in Jackson. Save for Miss Amy Dawson,' he added with a smile. 'I'll be back for her. Guess the whole town knows about the two of us.'

'I guess they do, Mr Harding.' Radman turned as the door from the street opened and Charlie and Bruno appeared with Lucy close behind. Charlie tugged at the

151

brim of his hat. 'Mornin, Doctor Radman.'

'What is it, Lucy?' Harding asked.

'A big box has just arrived next door, Mr Harding.'

'What's in it?'

Lucy shook her head. 'I don't know. It's all closed up.'

'OK, I'll take a look later.'

'A good girl, that Lucy,' Radman said, standing up after she had left. 'I'd better be getting back to Josh Wake.'

'How is he, Doc?'

'A darn sight better than I ever thought he'd be. Tells me he's gonna sit on his porch and smoke his pipe.' Radman smiled, the expression on his face prompting Harding to think the doctor wasn't telling him something. Maybe the lawyer was up and dancing a quadrille.

'Stage is comin' in, Mr Harding. We gonna meet it for the last time?'

'We sure are, Charlie.'

Harding picked up his hat, settled his gun-belt out of habit and together the two men walked out of the office and crossed Main Street heading towards the stage station.

'Folks are walkin' with a spring in their step,' remarked Charlie.

'They sure—'

Harding broke off as he saw two of the passengers step down from the stage on to the boardwalk. One was a very tall man wearing a dust coat, unbuttoned, over a city suit. As Harding watched, the newcomer took off his grey derby hat and brushed it with his hand before settling it back on his head. Alongside him, several inches shorter, stood a soldier, his uniform bearing a captain's insignia. Both the men looked around and exchanged a few words. Harding turned to Charlie.

'If I don't get a chance to say this afore I leave, Charlie, I wanna say I've been real proud to serve with you.'

'Them's mighty fine words, Mr Harding, an' I thank you for 'em. But why you sayin' such words right now?'

'I think those two men by the stage are here for me. They're gonna put me on this stage for Cheyenne where I was s'posed to be some weeks ago. C'mon, let's get it over with.'

Harding stepped up to the boardwalk, Charlie close behind with Bruno. The young captain sprung to attention and saluted. 'Captain Firth reporting, Colonel.'

'At ease, Captain, and it's major.' Harding smiled wryly in the direction of the taller man. 'At least for a few more days,' he added.

The young officer looked surprised. 'Sir, I didn't know the news had reached from Cheyenne. The general only posted your promotion a few days ago.'

Harding swallowed a couple of times before looking at the officer's companion. 'What's goin' on here, Zacharias?'

'The general wants you promoted afore you quit the Army. You're the toast of Governor Thayer's office, Clay. He's jumpin' around like a jackrabbit, you havin' found the gold. Says he's gonna be dinin' out on it for years!'

'Miss Amy Dawson found the gold,' Harding said quickly. 'I just happened to be along.'

Captain Firth looked at the sheet of paper in his hand. 'That's my next task, Colonel. I'm ordered to give Miss Dawson this paper so she may claim the reward. Do you know where I can find the lady?'

'She'll be in Bannon's hotel, an' you'll find a place there to wash off the trail dust.'

'I'll be stayin' until next week,' Zacharias Hogg said. 'The soldiers will be here today to pick up the gold. You can give me the full story of what's been goin' on here. Warden's brother needs to be told how Frank died. I hope you've been keepin' a full journal.'

'Every word's there, Zacharias. We'll let you an' the captain get cleaned up.'

'Did you see those two fancy dressed fellers get off the stage behind Mr Hogg?' Charlie asked when they'd got back to the office and he was pouring coffee for them both.

'Can't say I did,' admitted Harding. 'I was thinkin' more of my boss an' that cap'n.'

'You sure were, Colonel,' Charlie said. 'Guess I'm gonna have to salute you from now on.'

'I've only one good arm, Charlie Wilson, but I'm still sheriff an' I can still put you in the horse trough.'

They were both roaring with laughter when the door opened and to Harding's surprise, Henry Yorke and Beth Maynard entered the office. Still trying to control his laughter, Harding invited them both to sit down.

'Forgive us, Beth, you too, Mr Yorke,' Harding said, a broad smile still on his face. 'Me an' Charlie were just indulgin' in high jinks. What can I do for you?'

Beth Maynard and Yorke took the seats Charlie brought forward.

'Mr Harding,' Beth said, 'if I understand aright, now that my legal husband is dead under the law of Wyoming I inherit all his property.'

Harding thought for a moment. 'After women got the vote in 1869 married women also got the right to property. But Pierce's kinfolk would inherit, not you.'

'But supposin' he had no kinfolk. All his family died in the great fire of 1845.'

'Then you'd inherit if you could prove you were legally married.'

Beth's face went ashen. 'Omigod!' she screamed. She leapt to her feet and, picking up her skirts, ran out of the office. The three men were left staring at each other in

154

amazement. Even Bruno opened an eye.

'You know what this is all about, Mr Yorke?' Harding asked the rancher.

Yorke shrugged. 'All I know is Doc Radman allowed Beth to have a long talk with Josh Wake. She an' Miss Dawson were with him for nigh on an hour. But what they talked about beats me.'

'How come Miss Dawson got involved?'

'Beth said she wanted someone with her who was smart and that she could trust.'

The three men were silent for several minutes. Then the door flew open and Beth reappeared, clutching in front of her a single sheet of paper.

'I told Big Harry to burn everything,' she said, breathlessly. 'I forgot this was in the secretary.'

She sat down and handed the sheet of paper to Harding who recognized it immediately. It was a certificate issued in Pittsburgh to confirm a lawful marriage. The one he held bore the names of Jacob William Pierce and Elizabeth Ann Maynard. He looked up at Beth and smiled.

'You now own a saloon, a heap of grazing land, and some old coal tunnels.'

Beth let out a deep sigh. 'Exactly what Mr Wake told me!' She looked at the tiny watch pinned to her jacket. 'Miss Dawson will be here in a moment with two gentlemen,' she announced.

Charlie was faster than Harding. 'They just arrived on the stage?'

Beth nodded. 'They certainly did, Charlie Wilson.' She swung around in her seat. 'An' here they are.'

The door had opened as she spoke and Amy entered followed by the two men Charlie had noticed stepping down from the stage. Harding looked around the office. The place was getting crowded.

155

'Charlie, get a coupla chairs from the passageway.' He stood up and pushed his own chair around the desk so Amy could take a seat. As Charlie brought through chairs for the two newcomers, Harding shifted to sit on the corner of his desk.

'Mr Keen and Mr Johnson,' Beth announced. 'Sheriff Harding and Deputy Wilson,' she introduced them.

'How can we help you, gentlemen?' Harding asked.

Keen spoke first. 'Mr Johnson and I represent the Union Pacific Railroad Company. Coal companies have been charging us far too much for coal. So we're going to mine our own.'

'There's coal out by the river,' Harding said, 'an' I can't claim to know much about minin' but I'd have thought you needed more land.'

'You're right, Sheriff, so we're going to buy all the land owned by Miss Maynard, and we'll pay to shift all of Jackson Creek twenty miles along the river.'

'Jumpin' rattlesnakes!' Charlie exclaimed.

'Every store and home will be the same as here and the owners rewarded handsomely,' Beth said.

Harding tried not to show the doubt on his face. Beth seemed to believe that the arrival of UP and the move of Jackson could be achieved with a flick of a mare's tail. UP had been known to exploit naive settlers in the past and Mayor Bannon and the town's councillors would have to step carefully.

'We have the whole winter to plan,' said Johnson. 'Nothing will start until next spring, and then we shall start hiring men.'

'There's a bunch of ex-Navy men in town, they'd be good for you.'

'I can't see 'em working down below,' Johnson said, 'but we could sure use men like that above ground, and we can bring in our own miners.'

'Just hold it there, Mr Johnson.'

Harding pushed himself off the corner of his desk and crossed to the door leading to the passageway. Closing the door behind him he glanced at the three strongboxes stored in the cage opposite to Frenchie's. By the end of the day the Army would take on responsibility for the gold and he and Charlie could relax. He approached the cage where Frenchie, hammer in hand, was repairing a bar of the cage.

'Follow me, Frenchie, an' keep your wits about you,' Harding ordered. He pushed back into the office with Frenchie a couple of paces behind.

'This is Mr Dupont,' Harding announced. 'He did an important job for the Army a coupla weeks back.' He turned to Frenchie. 'How long were you minin' for, did you tell me?'

'Ten years, Mr Harding.'

The two UP men exchanged glances. 'Where were you mining, Mr Dupont?' Johnson asked.

'Pennsylvania for the whole ten years, diggin' hard coal. Last three as boss of forty men.'

'We'll take you on next spring,' said Johnson promptly.

'He can't wait for that,' cut in Harding. 'I was thinkin' I was gonna send him to Cheyenne.'

Again the two men exchanged glances. They must have reached some unspoken agreement for both of them nodded at the same time. 'Stay in town, and we'll put you on half-pay from tomorrow until next spring,' Johnson said. 'An' you'll earn it. We'll be sending men over here for short stays from next month. You gotta see they're taken care of.'

'I can do that,' said Frenchie. 'When it's slow this winter, is it OK to work at a store, here in town? I ain't gonna be paid for it, I'm just helpin' out.'

'We've no problem with that,' Johnson said. 'We've heard

about your winters and we'll not be around.'

'Carry on with that job, Frenchie,' Harding said. 'It seems to be goin' well.'

A broad grin spread across Frenchie's face as he turned away. 'Never better, Mr Harding.'

Keen and Johnson got to their feet. 'Seems we've gone as far as we can for now. The stage ain't gonna wait for ever,' Keen said. 'Miss Maynard, if you give me the name of your lawyer, we'll write to him.'

Beth smiled. 'Address your letter to Mr Clay Harding. He'll have an office in town.'

Harding was so shocked he almost slipped off the edge of his desk. What was Beth thinking of? He hadn't practised law for almost ten years. He knew nothing about mining law, land law in the Territory or a host of subjects a lawyer would need. The smart operators working for UP would stampede over him. With difficulty he maintained a calm expression as the two UP men shook hands with them all, and bowed to the ladies before leaving. Then Harding exploded.

'Are you crazy, Beth? I can't be your lawyer. Those rattlesnakes from UP would eat me alive! Sure, I know some law but it'll not stretch that far.'

'You've the whole winter to study, almost a year afore you have to make any decisions.'

'But I've no books, no experience of this type of law.'

'All the books you need are in a box next door,' said Amy quietly. 'Mr Wake is retiring and he's cleared his library. He said he'll guide you where necessary. Miller is leaving town on the stage. Clay, you'll be the lawyer for the new Jackson Creek.'

Beth leaned forward to grasp Yorke's hand. 'And I'll need you to register my marriage to Henry.' A smile played on her lips as she looked sideways at Amy. 'An' I guess you'll be registerin' your own.'

Charlie laughed aloud. 'You've been corralled, Colonel!'

Harding looked around at all the smiling faces, his eyes lingering on the happy sparkle of Amy's green eyes. 'I guess you've got me behind a five-bar gate!' His smile broadened. 'An' it feels mighty good.'